The Wild Country

Books by
LOUIS BROMFIELD

A MODERN HERO

TWENTY-FOUR HOURS

AWAKE AND REHEARSE

THE STRANGE CASE OF MISS ANNIE SPRAGG

A GOOD WOMAN

EARLY AUTUMN

POSSESSION

THE GREEN BAY TREE

THE FARM

HERE TODAY AND GONE TOMORROW

THE MAN WHO HAD EVERYTHING

THE RAINS CAME

IT TAKES ALL KINDS

NIGHT IN BOMBAY

WILD IS THE RIVER

UNTIL THE DAY BREAK

MRS. PARKINGTON

WHAT BECAME OF ANNA BOLTON

THE WORLD WE LIVE IN

PLEASANT VALLEY

A FEW BRASS TACKS

COLORADO

MALABAR FARM

THE WILD COUNTRY

The WILD COUNTRY

A NOVEL

BY

LOUIS BROMFIELD

HARPER & BROTHERS
NEW YORK

9 - 8

THE WILD COUNTRY

COPYRIGHT, 1948, BY LOUIS BROMFIELD

PRINTED IN THE UNITED STATES OF AMERICA

FIRST EDITION

H - X

The Wild Country

PART I

I HEARD OLD VIRGIL SAY, "HENRY'S BRUNG himself home a chippy." And my grandfather asked, "Where from?" And then Old Virgil said, "From the World's Fair. I always said country boys shouldn't be messin' around a place like that."

What I heard meant nothing to me at all and scarcely made an impression on my brain, and I went on playing with Prince who kept running after the sticks I threw for him and then coming back and jumping up with both paws on my shoulders. I wasn't much heavier than the old sheep dog, and each time he sprang at me in his excitement he nearly knocked me down; but it didn't matter because we understood each other. He had been my dog since I was not quite two years old when Henry's father had brought him over, a soft, fat, woolly puppy. Prince was twelve years old now but still strong and full of life. Each time he licked my face he made me laugh, and I kept laughing so hard, and Prince kept barking so hard that my grandfather turned away from Old Virgil and said sharply, "That's enough, Ronnie! I can't hear myself think! Go on down by the creek and play." And I knew by his voice and the way he spoke to me that he was worried or irritated by something. He was a calm man but when irritated or worried sometimes struck out at you when the cause had nothing whatever to do with you. It was as if the nerves and brain, usually so placid and controlled, grew suddenly taut to the point of breaking. Sometimes he struck thus out of irritation or impatience with stupidity or intolerance, and sometimes he hit not the object of his impatience but someone he loved who had nothing to do with the irritation.

So Prince and I left him talking to the old man and ran down the long slope in front of the Big House across the bluegrass until we came to the low ground along the creek where the mint and the sweet flag grew so thick that they caught and held my running feet and slowed my progress to a walk.

It was a warm, bright afternoon in late May, and the smell of mint and sweet flag crushed by my progress filled the air all about us. It was mixed too with other wonderful smells—the smell of the swiftly running creek where thousands of minnows lay in the clear water, noses up stream, flashing and glittering as the sun, piercing the spring water, struck their silvery scales. And there was the smell of the rich, black bogland that bordered the stream and even a whiff of the strong pungent smell of a skunk cabbage leaf bruised by one of us in our hurried progress. And we came presently to the edge of the creek and Prince, still barking, leapt from the high bank between the willows full into a pool, scattering both minnows and water which, flying high above him, glittered in the brilliant sunlight.

The dog stood there in the water barking up at me, begging me to throw another stick, but suddenly I was tired with that luxurious, soft weariness which comes suddenly over a growing boy when the warm sun of late spring starts all the wakening glands to work just as it starts the plants and trees to grow and blossom and carry on the whole cycle of life.

I lay down on the soft warm bank and presently there came over me a curious sense of being a part of all these things which surrounded me—a part of the little flashing stream and the scent of mint, of the sunlight and the lettuce-green willows. Prince was in it, too, not as an animal removed from me by barriers which somehow had come to separate man from the animals and bring him both arrogance and misery, but as a friend. And beyond him was the crying of the frogs and toads in the shallow, murky waters of the marshland behind us.

Lying there on the bank in the late spring sunlight, with my child's body growing and swelling and expanding, I felt a delight at the touch of the warm, fertile earth and a quick desire to press myself closer to it, as if to thus become more intimately a part of all the luxurious growth and awakening fertility which lay in the low, damp marshes all about me, in the bursting of the buds and the faint fragrance of the wild crab blossoms on a tree somewhere near by, unseen but endowed with the fragrance that led the bees straight from the hives behind the Big House a mile away toward the blossoms which each year they fertilized so that there would be the little sourish apples that in winter fed the raccoons, the rabbits, the muskrats and the birds. It was one of those moments which survive for years in the memory, perhaps because it seemed then and afterwards to be the apotheosis of delight in living when for a brief time one becomes a part of a pattern in which egotism and loneliness are alike annihilated.

And presently Prince, perhaps overcome by the voluptuousness of the soft air and the running water, stopped barking and stood there in the running water looking up at me with only his head emerging. And then I knew what I wanted to do. I wanted to join him there as if the water, running over my body, somehow would bring me nearer to the whole miracle of the earth coming back to life with the burgeoning of the new season. It was, of course, no more than the familiar impulse and the hunger of a small boy to go swimming for the first time during the awakening year, but in that impulse, common to all small, growing boys, there were all the forces of nature itself.

I sat up and began to strip off my clothes, and Prince, divining that I was about to join him, began again to bark and sprang up the bank shaking the spring water out of his shaggy coat over my bare body and my clothes. The water felt cold, so cold that for a moment I shivered in the warm sunlight. Then I slipped down the bank over the willow roots washed bare during the early spring floods onto the bank of sand which lay just below.

The sand was warm and felt good as it slipped between my toes, and lazily I lay down, hugging its warmth. As I lay there, naked, on my stomach, I discovered just beneath my freckled snub nose a whole universe of growing things. There were fresh young seedlings of marsh grasses and summer weeds and even a whole plantation of tiny sycamore trees, springing from a million seeds which only last autumn had been contained in a single ball of fluff, like the old-fashioned tassels on the curtains at the Big House. There were hundreds of them, but only one or two perhaps would survive to grow into the great white-trunked trees that spread their shade over the bottom pastures and were beautiful—in summer when the cows and horses stood in their thick, dark shade fighting flies and in winter when their bare white branches reached their arms high against the dark sky. Along the whole length of the creek until it reached the lake and the Wild Country, there were millions of these tiny seedlings, brought into being so that at least a dozen or more might survive.

And beyond the end of my nose lay the clear pool where Prince had been swimming. It was still again now and clear and undisturbed, all the murkiness washed away by the swift flowing current. I could see to the bottom where once again the glittering minnows, disturbed only momentarily by the exuberance of the big dog, had reformed themselves with almost military precision, their mouths pointing upstream to catch whatever food drifted past. Above them in the shallow swift-running shoal water lay a school of big fish, grey-green with touches of faded scarlet about their heads and their feathery fins. They were the big red-horse-suckers guarding the nests where the female had hollowed a depression in the gravel and deposited hundreds of thousands of eggs. The eggs, like the seeds of the sycamores, would burst presently and release into life hundreds of thousands of tiny minnows of which only a few score would survive to carry on the race of suckers which had survived out of the mists of a steaming, swampy past.

I knew about those suckers. I knew about them in two ways. My grandfather had told me all about them and their close connection with the remote past of the world, and I had read of them in the big thick books with colored plates which my Great Aunt Susan kept in her room and loaned to me one at a time. But I knew about them in another, perhaps better, fashion because in the warm spring nights I had gone out after it was dark with Henry Benson to pick them up quite easily off the shallow riffles where in their passion for reproduction they took no notice of us. I knew how their colors changed in breeding season and how, when the tiny fry were hatched, they disappeared to hide on the very bottom of the deep holes where it was almost impossible to catch them with ordinary bait. I knew about them in two ways, very different, as people sometimes knew about living, one kind cautiously out of books, as you might say, and the other kind by living.

What Henry and I did—picking up the dazed fish out of the shallow water—wasn't legal even in those far-off days, because it was too easy to pick up the dazzled fish swarming over the shoals, and it wasn't much sport. I think what Henry enjoyed was the feel of the warm spring nights when the red-horse-suckers were running and that sense of losing himself in the spring-scented infinite darkness. It was exciting and it made you feel good and when you went home to bed, there was peace in your head and you slept well in that deep sleep which is near to death and peace and to eternity itself.

In a little while I sat up and put one foot into the water. It was still cold but not so cold as one would have expected at that time of year. Prince, who had been lying beside me with his nose pressed against the warm sand, sat up and barked at me and then I stood up and dived into the pool among the shimmering minnows, striking out and splashing wildly to overcome the shock of the cold spring water. And then my body accustomed itself to the chill of the water, and when I was out of breath, I swam to the lower end of the pool and lay there on my back, letting the water flow over my naked body.

In a little while the silvery minnows regained their formation and, sitting up, with only my shoulders out of the water, I watched them holding their position against the current with almost imperceptible movements of fins and tail. After a little while a few of the smaller ones, which seemed all of a special kind, moved away and came toward me, nibbling at my toes and then at my bare legs, and the nibbling together with the movement of the water over my body, filled me with a curious, yearning sensuality, for what I did not know, save that somehow it too was a part of the warm sun, the scent of crushed mint, the nesting fish and the perfume of the wild crab apple blossoms.

Beside me, in the shallower water a hellgrammite slipped out from under a rock and made a perilous, skittering journey to another shelter a little way off, and a crayfish crept out of the water and slipped into one of the dark holes in the rich soil of the stream bank. A pair of killdeer, with a nest somewhere in the near-by pasture, made a teetering progress across the gravel bank till Prince saw them and drove them again high into the blue sky, uttering wild plaintive cries.

Then slowly I lay down again in the shallow pool with only my head emerging, with nothing above me but a brilliant blue sky, spotted here and there with cool, small, cottony clouds and gave myself up to thoughts about my grandfather, about Old Virgil, about Great Aunt Susan and the Big House on the shelf of land halfway up the long hill.

I heard again Old Virgil saying, "Henry has brung himself home a chippy." And I wondered why Henry had had to go all the way to St. Louis to get himself a chippy when the fence-rows over all the farm were full of them, and I could see them in my imagination, little and grey, like house wrens, with flirting tails. They nested among the young sassafras and wild cherry and elderberry that grew along the fence and the edge of the woods. They were hard to catch, but if Henry had wanted one bad enough to go all the way to the World's Fair for it, he could have made a little snare and caught one right here on the farm. It seemed a silly business.

And then I began to think about Henry himself. He was a strong wiry fellow, dark and blue-eyed, about twenty-three with dark curling hair cut short and a skin that was white as milk when he went swimming, except on his forearms and where he left his shirt open at the throat in summer, and he had a very powerful body, with big thighs and big arms and white shoulders. My grandfather always said he looked like Michelangelo's "David," but his strength wasn't a clumsy strength, he moved like a panther and he always seemed to be in a hurry, except on the Sunday afternoons when he went swimming or fishing and on those nights when he followed the coon dogs through the swamps and the thickets. My grandfather said that he was the best man he had ever seen with animals and that he was the best man he had ever seen on a farm.

I liked to think about Henry, for to a boy of thirteen, he seemed to me to know everything that it was of any use for anyone to know. He always knew when the wild ducks would appear on the marshes, and the location of every fox lair, and he would sit up all night with a sick colt or calf, and he knew the pools in the Clear Fork where the big smallmouthed bass hid away. He was born in that county, of its earth and its wooded hills and springs and marshes. As I lay there with the cool water running over me, he seemed a part of that world in which I had lost myself. He was a hero to me, a hero like Jason or David or Richard Coeur de Lion. I would be like Henry when I grew up and maybe someday when grandfather died and I took over all these big farms we could work together there, side by side.

When I was born Henry was ten years old, and as I grew up he had taken me on as a kind of charge, teaching me things, letting me follow him around, answering all the endless questions of a child discovering the world. I know now that the relationship was less unusual than it might appear, for we lived in the country where differences in age mean less and we were nearer together in mind than one would expect, for Henry had had only a simple schooling and I was a precocious boy with a mind packed with facts and information. In the question of the red-horse-suckers, he could show me everything about the way they lived and reproduced, but I could tell him about their relation to the past and how fish had become reptiles and reptiles had become birds. He would listen, fascinated, and say, "Well, Bud, that's the most interesting thing I ever heard!"

I think my grandfather encouraged our relationship for two reasons, because, being so much older than myself, my ceaseless questioning bored him and because he thought Henry was an excellent companion for a growing boy. There weren't any Boy Scouts in those days but Henry was a whole troop in himself.

And I found myself thinking too of Old Virgil, so gnarled and shrunken, with one eye that trailed off at an angle so that you could never tell which eye to look into when he talked to you. Old Virgil belonged there in the Valley too. He was as much a part of it as Henry, but he was different—gossipy and spiteful and trouble-making as if there were something inside him which was perpetually snarling and gnawing. I couldn't think why he should mind so much because Henry had brought a little chippy sparrow home from the World's Fair. It seemed to hurt Old Virgil and make him angry and happy at the same time.

Then I heard the bell ringing from the Big House and knew that probably Old Virgil had gone away and that grandfather wanted me at the house to go on with my lesson in Greek.

So I left the pond and put my clothes on over my wet body, reluctantly, because I was returning out of that vast world in which I had been wandering about—a vast, infinite world of daydreaming in which I was lost and insignificant and happy—

back into the finite world of the Big House, lessons in Greek, of supper with Great Aunt Susan complaining that my hands and ears were not clean enough.

When I had dressed, Prince and I set out again across the warm, scented mint beds and across the meadow where the cows lay munching the blue-grass and white clover, up the long slope toward the Big House with its turrets and cupolas surrounded by locust and black walnut trees. I walked slowly, scuffing my feet, kicking and scattering the heaps of dried cow dung to spread them out as I had seen Henry, as a good farmer, do so often. Prince would have scuffed his paws as well if he could have done so. The fun had gone out of him too at the prospect of returning to the ordered life of the Big House. And all the while I kept thinking about Henry and wondering why he had to go all the way to St. Louis to get a chippy.

It was all like that. Now, two generations after-ward, the memory of that afternoon is still fresh and brilliant in my mind. Perhaps because as one grows older one remembers more and more clearly things that happen in very early childhood, and perhaps more because one never forgets things which have to do with love and growth and the primitive forces of creation and reproduction and immortality. I think that the warm spring afternoon marked in a way the beginning of my adolescence and the first stirrings in my childish body of all those forces which can bring so much delight and so much sorrow, which determine in the end what our lives shall be. I remember it all clearly too because it was all associated with Henry Benson and with the mysterious chippy he had brought back from St. Louis, for it was through them that I learned as I grew into young manhood many of the things concerning love and life and immortality which gave me an understanding of what I was and how I fitted into the universal scheme of things. If one has a reflective temperament, the things which touch one's growth and understanding are not quickly forgotten but return again and again to the very end of life.

The Big House toward which I hurried across the meadows sat on a hill overlooking the whole valley. It was a tall, complicated house with turrets and a high-roofed piazza that ran around three sides of it, an ugly house which on that site would have been a sore thumb save for the great trees —a mixture of elms and black walnuts and locust, and apple trees which surrounded it. Beyond the encircling trees lay a wide stretch of closely clipped lawn with two cast-iron stags, always freshly whitewashed each summer, which looked out over the valley from between circular flower beds planted with a brilliant mixture of kohlias, salvia, begonia and geraniums. Unlike the Valley and the country-side there was nothing wild about the house or its immediate surroundings. Everything was orderly, clipped, subdued and neat, as befitted the country place of a well-to-do and distinguished man who had been a senator, a judge, and an ambassador.

Beyond the lawns, white painted fences separated the paddocks where in summer, deep in bluegrass and white clover, grazed the famous trotting horses which my grandfather bred. These paddocks joined the big barns and stables where in winter the horses lived in big roomy stalls. At one end was the dairy and the stalls belonging to the sleek, black-faced, sloe-eyed Jersey cows and their master, a ferocious Jersey bull called Magnificent Oliver of Clarendon. Beyond that stood the cabins of the Negro grooms and stable boxes built around a square with a well and chain pump in the center. From the barns and stables past the tall, ugly house surrounded by trees ran a white ribbon of lane leading down to the county road. Where the lane joined the road there was a great archway with the name "Clarendon Stock Farm" in iron letters. On pillars on each side of it, like the gods of the place, were cast-iron figures of a trotting stallion and a Jersey bull. The whole place had been built a little while after the Civil War with the money my grandfather inherited from his father.

By the time I reached the house and my grandfather's study on that hot May day, I was out of breath. My grandfather looked at me sternly and asked, "Where were you? Did you forget the hour?"

I told him I was sorry and I didn't tell him that from the moment I had left him and Old Virgil talking at the head of the lane, I had been lost in dreams, drifting through the whole of the universe. I could not explain. The lesson in Greek was the only thing he asked of me in return for the long summers of delight spent each year at Clarendon Farm.

His study was a cool, high-ceilinged room with tall uncurtained windows. In place of curtains there were multiple paneled shutters which folded back into the window frames. In a house built in the rich Mississippi basin they were excellent for admitting air and keeping out the brilliant sun of midsummer. The walls were lined with bookshelves, most of them filled with books on international law, history and biography which my grandfather had moved down from his big house in St. Louis as he grew older and came to spend more and more time at the stock farm. In the open spaces on the wall there were engraved portraits of George Washington and Abraham Lincoln and in a niche over the big desk a copy of a Houdon bust of Voltaire.

It was a room which fitted my grandfather. Its high ceilings suited a man so tall and lean. It was austere and dignified and yet warm.

I liked my grandfather. Because my own parents had both been drowned in the sinking of the Calpurnia on their way home from Europe when I was not quite two years old, I had lived always with grandfather and his maiden sister, known to me as "Aunt Susan." Although sixty years separated us, my grandfather and I got on very well. I think he had never forgotten what it was like to be a boy. Sometimes when we met for a walk across the fields to see the mares and foals, he would quietly take my hand in his as we walked. It never annoyed me as it might have annoyed some small boys or as it might have done if he had been another person. It was a simple, old-fashioned gesture of affection which gave me pleasure and somehow bridged that wide gap of sixty years and brought us nearer to each other.

He had a lean face with very young dark eyes, a straight nose and a wide, rather full mouth. The height of his brow and the breadth of his temples asserted an intellectual quality that seemed at variance with the rather full sensual mouth; yet taken together the two indicated intelligence and vigor and made him an extraordinarily handsome man. He was also, perhaps because of his frank direct masculine beauty, a man whom people liked and trusted. He had been upright and uncompromising even in politics. He had been in his long day a judge, a senator and an ambassador, and now he was through with it all and spent more and more time at the stock farm with his beloved trotting horses and his pretty black-faced sloe-eyed Jerseys.

The lesson in Greek that day was a long passage from Xenophon and it went badly. I was still a little lost in the haze which had come over me beside the clear little creek, and I found myself still thinking about my hero Henry and the chippy he had brought home from the World's Fair. I struggled along stupidly and after about half an hour my grandfather said, "Never mind, son. Your heart isn't in it today. If your heart isn't in it, nothing sticks to the brain."

He always called me "son" or "Ronnie" and in turn I called him "Grandad."

He looked at me grinning and said, "Something's troubling you. What is it?"

I said, "What did Old Virgil mean when he said Henry had brung home a chippy?"

There was a quick twinkle in the dark eyes and then his face grew sober. He was silent for a moment and he said, "I think Old Virgil had his information mixed up. I don't believe Henry brought home a chippy."

"Is there any other kind of chippy than a sparrow?"

He smiled again. "I'm afraid there is." He took off his steel-rimmed glasses and rubbed his eyes for a moment. Then he looked directly at me and said, "I guess you'll understand if I tell you. Anyway you're getting old enough to know. The other kind of chippy is a bad woman, son. You know all about breeding horses and cows and I guess you must know that's how people get children. Well, the kind of bad woman people call a 'chippy' is the kind of woman who just goes about breeding with men—any kind of men—without marrying them. Sometimes she doesn't even really know them. She just does it for money and sometimes for pleasure. She doesn't do it out of love or to have children. Usually, it's a pretty good idea to keep away from women like that."

Seated on the edge of my chair, I listened, confused by the variety of my emotions. I was pleased that my grandfather was treating me like a grown-up man, and I was fascinated by what he was telling me because it made clear many things which until that moment had existed in a fog of confusion compounded of things I had read precociously in books, of fragments of overheard conversations, of things I had heard from the older boys at boarding school. But I was troubled too about Henry and even a little jealous that he had married and brought home a wife. Now he wouldn't have as much time for me. He wouldn't take me swimming or spearing suckers in the creek. In spite of my grandfather's treating me like a grown man I felt the color rising in my face. I did not know why but I could not control it.

He went on gravely. "You understand what I mean? God and nature meant all things to multiply and increase and all of the higher animals as you well know, accomplish this in the same fashion. Man is endowed with special gifts and qualities which should make him wise in these things; but he isn't always wise and sometimes he is pretty much of an animal. He tries to pretend he isn't but sometimes it gets the best of him. You'll understand these things yourself in a few years. When a man or woman isn't wise, he or she usually pays for it. Do you understand now what a chippy is?"

"Yes."

"But I still don't think Henry brought home a chippy. In any case we'll drive over tomorrow and meet his new wife. Would you like that?"

"Yes, Grandad."

But I wasn't really sure. It was still hurting me that Henry could go off like that and forget me and bring home a woman and not tell me anything about it. I kept thinking of Henry as something different and strange—now that he would be living with a woman I had never seen. I felt that he must have changed, but I did not know why. The woman might not like me, and I was sure I wouldn't like her. I thought bitterly that very probably she *was* a chippy, although that thought somehow defiled the clean, shining picture of Henry himself. And somewhere in the back of my mind were confused images of the stallions, rearing and crying out as if they were in pain as Red McGovern led them into the paddock to breed the mares. I felt suddenly confused and depressed.

My grandfather rose and said, "You'd better go and wash up for supper."

As I turned to go, he said, "You mustn't worry too much about what I told you. If anything puzzles you, just ask me and we'll straighten it out. You're older for your years than most boys and you know more, because you've lived in the country. And remember all these things are in a way nature—sometimes just a part of the folly and compulsions of mankind. So don't take any of it too seriously."

He always talked to me thus, using big words as if I were his equal, never talking down to me. No father could have done better. Indeed, no father could perhaps have done it so well, because, as I know now my grandfather's great age and experience and wisdom and his own tragedy had helped him to tolerance and to simplicity and utter honesty. He only told me what I already knew in a vague, confused fashion but he did it so that it all seemed as simple and natural as the rising of the sun.

But I still couldn't understand about Henry. If he'd meant to bring back a wife he'd have told me before he went to St. Louis. Maybe, I thought, he'd just found her there unexpectedly or maybe it was that odd thing they called "love at first sight" which I'd read about in books. It seemed to trouble my grandfather too for he said, "Funny he didn't tell us anything about it." And I suspected that he felt hurt because the news had come to him first from Old Virgil instead of from Henry himself.

As my grandfather grew older he came to spend more and more time at the stock farm and less and less time in St. Louis and Washington. He had always led a very active life and traveled much and I think he came presently to find no need for change or travel because he discovered the whole of the universe in the pattern of the farm and the Valley. His life at Clarendon Farm was like a second blossoming of an old tree which as the winter of death approaches puts forth pale and delicate flowers during the month of November. On the farm and in the Valley he discovered a small world in which all the parts and manifestations of the great world which he had known so well were repeated in a smaller, more intimate

22

pattern. He had always known the great things in life and now after the age of seventy, he had time to know and understand and value the small things which are in the end, perhaps, the key to all else. He found a warm delight in the sight of the young foals, in the blossoming of the orchards, in the affairs of the little township bank, in exchanging gossip with the postman, in going to the County Fair and to the lawn suppers of the Valley church.

Except for an occasional trip to Washington, he no longer went anywhere or visited anyone. He preferred to stay at the farm and have old friends or the old men with whom he had business come there to stay with him.

Nearly always there was someone staying in the Big House or sometimes many people. Occasionally they stayed overnight and sometimes they came just for a meal—politicians, horse breeders, farmers, bankers, professors, lawyers. Twice while I was a boy, Presidents of the United States stopped at Clarendon Farm. We had only one visitor who ever stayed for more than a day or two. He was a protégé of my grandfather, a big attractive man called Wayne Torrance. He was the son of a poor neighboring farmer whom my grandfather had helped through school and later taken into his law firm.

But on that particular evening there were no visitors and only grandfather, Aunt Susan and myself sat at the big mahogany table served by Jackson Winters. Jackson was a very old Negro who had worked for my grandfather almost the whole of both their lives. He was bent and his kinky hair had long since turned white and he was quite deaf. As a young man he had been a slave and there was about him a great deal of the old-fashioned "darky." For me, at least, he was as much an integral and indispensable part of the big Ulysses S. Grant house as my grandfather and Aunt Susan or my grandfather's library or the big mahogany table. His deafness, my grandfather found, was no fault; rather it was a convenience because my grandfather and his friends could gossip or talk of secret and confidential things in front of Jackson without his ever hearing. If my grandfather wanted to make Jackson hear, he simply addressed him, without raising his voice, in the queer flat and penetrating tone used by deaf people. My grandfather's natural voice was warm and rather deep and the change from his own voice to the one he used in talking with Jackson had the queer, uncalculated effect of ventriloquism and never ceased to cause in me a wild desire to laugh.

The dining room was a distinctly "grand" room, large and high with tall windows running from floor to ceiling and opening onto the big piazza. The walls were papered with pale grey, overlaid with arabesques of gold and at the

24

high windows hung beneath ornate gilt balde-
quins long crimson curtains which were tied back
with gold cords. There was nothing "country" or
"chintzy" about the room or about the whole
house. I understood from grandad's and Aunt
Susan's casual conversation that "Melissa" had
been responsible for the curtains and indeed the
decorations of the whole house. The curtains were
faded at the edges, yet they still possessed an air
of grandeur and luxury. Between them through
the high windows there was a long, lovely view
of the Valley with its streams and green fields and
woods toward the wild hill country which lay just
beyond in a haze of pale grey blue. All that wild
distant hill country was forbidden to me and
Prince on our ramblings. Grandfather was afraid
we might lose ourselves in it. And so to me it remained a romantic, mysterious region. The only
people who lived there lived in cabins and came
only occasionally into the county seat on Saturday nights, where they stood about, the men lank
and bearded, the women clad in cheap shapeless
dresses holding one child by the hand and carrying another.

When we were alone my grandfather sat at the
head of the long table and his sister Susan at the
far end. I was placed somewhere in between.

Aunt Susan was a small, thin wisp of a woman
who could never have weighed as much as a hun-

dred pounds in all the time I knew her. She was a brisk, little person and dressed in a brisk and practical fashion, usually in the daytime in an ankle-length skirt and a stiff and immaculate white shirt-waist with a high, starched collar. In the evenings she wore soft and lacy dresses in pale shades of green or mauve with lace yokes and high-boned collars. She was a great authority on the native birds and had written two books on the subject published originally at my grandfather's expense but later taken over by a publishing house because of their value and steady sale. She had never married although she must have been very pretty as a girl. To this day I do not know the reason. When "Melissa" left, Aunt Susan took over as hostess and housekeeper for her brother. She spent a great deal of the day roaming the woods and valleys sometimes driving one of grandfather's brood mares in a sulky, sometimes on foot. Like many very small, apparently frail people, she had great reserves of energy. Throughout the Valley and in the village she was known simply as "Miss Susan" although a few old women who had known her since my great-grandfather's day when she was a small girl, called her Susie. Her ramblings in the Valley were mostly concerned with bird watching and she always carried with her a pair of powerful field glasses slung over one shoulder and a tiny box of water colors with which she made intricate but beautifully executed pictures of the birds she saw or the nests she discovered. One had the feeling that her small, delicate body had some affinity with the birds themselves, as if in some earlier incarnation she had been a bird and never quite lost a nostalgic desire to rejoin them. Nevertheless she was an excellent and businesslike housekeeper and had taught Jackson's wife to make all sorts of foreign dishes which she had learned in Europe.

I must say that both grandfather and Aunt Susan were civilized people. When we were alone at dinner neither of them "made" conversation if they had nothing to say, but when they did talk the conversation was good, sometimes small talk, but more often talk of economics or politics or ornithology or of the great changes that were coming into the world—changes which I gathered had contributed much toward their longer and longer stay at Clarendon Stock Farm where they could keep the world, in which they had both lived and which they both loved, intact and unviolated. Sometimes one had the impression that they were both tired and that the quiet of the sleepy valley was a prelude to the death which they both regarded with indifference, like the birds or the great oaks or the forest, neither welcoming nor dreading it.

From the time I was old enough to talk, they listened with attention to what I had to say, as if I were a grown-up, and they never dampened the enthusiasm of a child in the process of discovering an immense and fascinating world, although at times my outbursts must have bored them. I learned much more at that table than I ever learned at school or even at the university.

They talked freely in front of me when I was very small and continued to do so even after I had grown older and had begun to understand far more of what they said than they ever suspected. Much of the talk was about the trotting horses and the intricacies and details of breeding, all of which Aunt Susan knew quite as well as my grandfather. Although the men at the stables would have as soon killed themselves as to permit a lady within half a mile of the stables on the mornings when mares from neighboring farms were brought over to be bred. Aunt Susan and my grandfather discussed the details quite frankly and dispassionately as if they were talking of chemical reactions in a laboratory. To me as a small boy, stallions and mares and the difficulties of their courtships and matings were as commonplace and natural as talk of the crops.

But they failed to understand fully the precociousness of a small boy and that I began to piece things together out of the fragments of their conversations as my wisdom and knowledge increased. That was how I came to guess rightly that "Melissa" was my grandmother.

For a great many years I had overheard talk of Melissa and a gentleman whom I never heard mentioned by name. He was known simply as "He." I never betrayed my growing knowledge to either of them, not because I wanted to continue eavesdropping, but because I felt that they *wanted* to believe that I did not understand what they were talking about and that if they ever suspected, it would hamper the freedom of their conversation and somehow alter the pleasant relationship among the three of us.

I do not know the exact moment when it dawned upon me that the mysterious Melissa was my grandmother. Somehow I simply came to know it, accepting the knowledge with the complete reasonableness of a child to whom, in an awakening world, still unhampered by conventions, few things are startling and everything is of equal importance and value.

On that night at dinner, there was in the conversation nothing new or especially revealing. For long periods I was lost in my own thoughts, still troubled by the news of the chippy Henry had brought home from the World's Fair. I knew that what my grandfather had told me in his study was not to be brought up before Aunt Susan; it was a conversation between men. And as I sat there I began to hate more and more the chippy whom I had never seen because she had come between me and my hero, Henry.

I do remember my grandfather saying, "I had a letter from Melissa today. 'He' is quite ill."

Aunt Susan asked, "Did she say what it was?"

"I gathered it must be his liver. They've gone to Bad Gastein."

"What else did Melissa say?"

"Nothing much."

"They're not coming back to America?"

"No."

Then Aunt Susan sighed, a curious deep sigh, filled with all the sadness in the world. For some reason I had expected my grandfather to sigh, but almost at once I realized that in all my short life I had never once heard my grandfather sigh. I knew suddenly that he could not sigh, that there were no sighs in him. He was not that kind of man.

That was all they said. There was a long silence and then my grandfather said, "Ronnie and I are going to drive over in the morning to meet Henry's new wife. Do you want to go along?"

Aunt Susan said, "No. There's too much to do around the house in the mornings. Besides I think it would be better if I went over alone. I think it would help if I made a formal, dressed-up call."

I saw my grandfather smile at her and I knew at the same time that she was in on the secret of the chippy. I heard him say, "I think that's an excellent idea."

30

Aunt Susan said, "You might drop a hint that I'll be over about four o'clock. I expect she'll want to know that I'm coming. What mare shall I take?"

My grandfather said, "Take Butterball but don't push her. She's due to foal in a week and some exercise will do her good."

Then Jackson brought in the coffee and I went off up to my room to read *Twenty Thousand Leagues under the Sea*. I was in the midst of the book and found it passionately exciting but somehow, that night, I couldn't keep my interest fixed upon it.

From my window I could see the whole of the Valley and even a bit of the big lake far down the Valley in the Wild Country and I found myself slipping away from the book again and again to watch the changing colors of the landscape as the sun went down. The clouds, hurrying over the Wild Country, turned pink and then a flaming red, and the blue and purple of the distant, wooded hills grew deeper and deeper as the sun slipped beneath the horizon. As it grew dark, I heard the distant amorous neigh of a stallion in the stables and on the ridge beyond the big house a dog-fox began to bark, and presently I was lost again in the daydreaming which had overtaken me beside the pool in the thicket.

I was aware, in a curious blurred fashion, that I knew many things which I did not understand and could not explain to myself. In the daydreams the figures of my grandfather, of Henry, of Melissa and "He," of the chippy were all blurred, yet real. None of them but my grandfather and Henry had I ever seen, yet in a way I felt a part of them and their lives and an awareness that what they were and what they knew were a part of all that lay before me. I would one day live as they had lived or were living. And again I experienced the strange sensation of growing, of actually feeling the muscles of my thighs and arms expanding, of forces working deeply and passionately inside me. I was filled with a sensation of richness and warmth. It was like the swelling of a bud beneath the warm sun of early spring.

A little while after breakfast my grandfather and I set out behind an old stallion called Ben Drake. He was a big chestnut horse and a great favorite of my grandfather, partly I think because he had had a noble career and won many races on the Grand Circuit and partly because there was a curious love between the two of them. Ben Drake had long since been retired from racing although, because of his record and his blood, he still served occasionally at stud for large fees. Save when he was out at pasture he got all his exercise by being driven about the countryside by his owner.

My grandfather had no fear of horses and had a fine hand with them. On that morning, despite

his age, Ben was full of spirit and not above playing tricks. As a horse he had a great deal of personality, almost one might have said, the sense of
humor of a practical joker. He would play-act at
times, shying at things invisible to his driver, or
at times bare his teeth and put on a show of feroc-
ity which only those who knew him best recognized as a fraud. Often enough when Ben was
showing off in one of his tantrums, I saw my
grandfather walk up to the stallion who was neighing, kicking, baring his teeth and tap him gently
on the nose saying, "Come on, Ben. Quit that! I
know all your tricks." And the horse would quiet
down at once. He would bully any man or horse
who didn't call his bluff.

It was a cool morning, and Ben was showing
off, and my grandfather, as we drove off, began
talking to him. The old gentleman had a special
voice with animals, warm and confident and caressing. He talked to them all from Prince, the Border
collie, up to Ben, the stallion, as if he really believed they understood everything he said, and perhaps they did. I know that the smartest dogs in the
world always belong to people who treat them as
equals. That was the way grandad treated all
animals and they responded to the treatment. There
was a curious tenderness in his voice that seemed to
pour out in his relationship to all animals, as if
somewhere at sometime in his relation with hu-

mans, he had been hurt and the natural outpouring of tenderness had been checked and dammed up to overflowing.

Now he talked to the old stallion, "Now Ben! I know your tricks! Take it easy. You're not fooling me. You needn't show off. We both know you. You're not as young as you once were. *I* know you're nineteen years old. You're no two-year old!"

He talked to the horse without self-consciousness, exactly as if I were not there at all or as if I understood exactly what he was doing. Then as we turned onto the county road he said, "All right, old fellow. Let her go! Show us what you can do." And he gave the old horse his head and let him go. For about a half mile we whizzed along the road, and then Old Ben had enough and he slowed down to a gentle trot like a well-mannered gelding.

I couldn't blame the horse for feeling well. The fence-rows on either side of the road were bright with clover and there was a faint scent of honeysuckle just beginning to flower on the steep banks. Where the sun had not yet touched the earth, the dew still glistened on the spider webs in the deep, fragrant timothy. In the pastures, the bluegrass and white clover grew rank and deep and in the wheat fields the grain was just beginning to shoot up into heads. The new, tender young corn stood lettuce-green in neatly cultivated rows.

But in spite of the beauty of the morning I was troubled and my uneasiness increased as we neared Henry's farm. I kept trying to imagine the scene of our meeting. I knew there would be a difference and with a child's instinct I knew that both Henry and I would recognize the fact and then try to pretend that nothing had changed. Somehow until now, I had never thought of him as being much different in age, although actually ten years separated us. But I knew that by bringing home a woman, he had become a man and that had changed everything. It was an experience which I could not possibly share with him and it would set up a barrier between us. From now on he would be a man and I'd be only a boy. It was worse too because he had brought home a chippy. By now after much brooding and some jealousy and perhaps because I wanted to believe it, I believed that Old Virgil had told the truth.

Henry lived in the big brick house on the farm he had inherited on the death of his widowed mother. It stood on a little rise above the road with a short lane bordered by big black locust trees that led up the slope in a curve past the stone springhouse built into the side of the hill. The spring was the biggest in the whole valley and from it flowed a whole brook of clear icy water that fed a little pond clotted by wild cress and bordered by wild yellow iris which were in flower that morn-

35

ing. The big red barn stood a little way from the house with the barnyard enclosed by a neat, white, painted wooden fence. In the brilliant early morning light, the buildings and even the individual leaves of the trees stood out clearly like the buildings and leaves in a Currier & Ives farm print.

As we reached the top of the drive, we saw Henry and his new wife coming out of the barn toward the house. She was carrying two metal milk pails and, with a pang of jealousy, I realized that she had been feeding the calves—a task which I had always done on the occasions when I had spent the night with Henry and helped with the chores in the morning.

She was young but she wasn't pretty. She was strongly built with a rather broad face, wide at the cheekbones, but her hair was wonderful, of a brilliant, golden yellow color. She was dressed in a clean checked gingham dress that came to the tops of her citified high button shoes. I wondered if all chippies looked like her, so that you could always recognize a chippy when you saw one.

Then as Henry saw us, he came forward smiling, saying something over his shoulder to the woman. Grandad pulled up Old Ben and held out his hand and said, "Well, Henry! Congratulations!"

They shook hands while I waited in a kind of dull misery. Then Henry turned toward me and shook my hand and said, "Well, Ronnie, it's been a long time since we've had a good fishing expedition."

It had happened then as I was afraid it would happen. He spoke to me as a man speaks to a child, almost condescendingly, and what he really said was, "I'm afraid, Ronnie, that our fishing expeditions are over now I'm a married man." And I was aware, rightly I think, that there was a change in him which I could not quite define, except that it had to do with what had happened to him since we had last met.

I felt the sting of childish tears under my eyelids and was ashamed of myself and I suddenly hated the strange woman who had come up to us and was now standing beside the dogcart.

Henry said, "This is my wife, Vinnie. This is Judge Stillcombe." Then he turned to me and said to her, "This is my old friend, Ronnie!" It was exactly as if he had patted me on the head.

The bitter thing was that he had never looked so much the picture of a small boy's hero. He wore a freshly washed pair of work pants with a blue shirt open at the throat and the sleeves rolled up well above the elbows. He had remarkable good looks with his dark hair and tanned skin and blue eyes with the long dark lashes. But there was nothing soft about him. The body beneath the work clothes was hard as iron.

And then I glanced at the woman, almost against

37

my will as if I could not help it. There was certainly nothing really pretty about her, yet I think I was aware even then of a kind of indefinable and changeable beauty, much deeper and more important than mere prettiness.

She put down the milk pails to take my grandfather's hand. She did not offer to shake hands with me but only smiled and said, "Pleased to meet you." And I was aware suddenly that she talked differently from us. It was not only that she had a faint accent but that her voice seemed different from the voices of our part of the country. It was plain that she was shy and that she had dreaded this meeting. She flushed as Henry introduced her and afterward stood there shyly and awkwardly with her hands rolled up peasant fashion in the clean apron she wore.

And then I noted that her hair wasn't really golden at all. At the roots where it had grown out an inch or two it was just plain brown.

Henry said, "Better stay a while. The chores are done and we've got some fresh buttermilk and that's what you like."

He went up to Old Ben's head and started to lead the horse across the few feet that separated us from the hitching rail under the maple trees. Over his shoulder he said, in his warm, slow voice, "Vinnie, go and fetch the buttermilk out of the springhouse."

38

She went away obediently down the steep stone steps to the moss-covered springhouse and grandad and I got out. For me, even the house and white picket fence which I knew so well, suddenly seemed changed and strange, as if my grandfather and I were visiting the place for the first time.

Then Henry said, "I guess it's kind of a surprise to you. I was goin' to drive over this evening and tell you the news. You see, it was kind of unexpected. I didn't even suspect it myself." The color showed suddenly in his face, even under the deeply tanned skin. "I couldn't come over the first night we got home."

My grandfather chuckled and said, "Well, I should hope not."

Henry led us up to the big, cool verandah and the rocking chairs Henry's mother had bought just before she died, and a second silence came over us. Then the girl came up the steps from the springhouse carrying a pitcher filled with buttermilk and the three of us watched her silently as she passed the corner of the house to fetch glasses. When she had disappeared, my grandfather said, "I suppose it'll seem pretty good to have a woman around the house again." And once more I felt a childish pang of jealousy. After Henry's mother died I had often spent the night in the house and in the morning helped Henry get breakfast and wash up. Now all that was over too.

"It sure is," said Henry. "Saves me a lot of time. Keeping bachelor's hall wasn't so good."

"Too bad you didn't get married here in the Valley. Susan and I would have given you a wedding party."

Henry didn't answer at once. He looked down at his big hands and then said, "Well, she wanted the weddin' in St. Louis. But thanks just the same." And even *I* knew Henry was lying. He couldn't tell a lie without becoming embarrassed.

"Susan wants to come over this afternoon and call on the new Missus," my grandfather said. "I suppose it'll be all right."

"Oh sure," said Henry, but without any show of enthusiasm. And then his wife came out with the buttermilk on a tray with glasses. She put the glasses on the table and filled them and stood back, watching us. There was something strange about her, very strange in our Valley. Any of our farm women would have pulled up a chair, sat down and begun gabbing right away.

Henry looked up at her and said, "Sit down, Vinnie." And you could see by his look that he had a passion for her. All the time we talked, he kept watching her. I had never noticed a man in love before but because the man was Henry and it made a great difference to me my eyes and ears grew sharp. It was very odd to see that look in Henry's face. I had seen him with girls at picnics and church suppers before, but I never saw him like this. He had always treated girls casually, joining in the fun but never settling to any one of them. And it wasn't because they didn't try to catch him. He was well-off and good-looking with the kind of looks which excited women and he owned five hundred acres of good Valley land. Some of them would have gone the whole way and caught him in a shot-gun wedding if it had been possible. That happened often enough in the Valley when young folks couldn't wait, or a girl wanted to catch a good husband.

The girl never said anything at all save when my grandfather addressed her and then she would smile in an embarrassed way and say "yes" or "no."

We left at last down the lane behind Old Ben and as we turned into the road I looked back and saw the two of them standing on the verandah. Henry's arm was about her waist. When I looked back at my grandfather, his face was serious, almost grim. I started to speak and then held my tongue, unwilling to break in upon his preoccupation.

On the way home all the rambunctiousness was gone out of Old Ben and we went slowly, in tempo with the curious mood of depression which had settled over both of us. It was odd. We had gone to call on a young couple just married and should have come away in high spirits.

And then as we crossed the covered bridge and came out at Old Virgil Plotz' farm, Old Virgil himself was crossing the road from his big red barn to the house. At sight of us he stopped by the side of the road, waiting.

Grandad pulled up Old Ben and we exchanged greetings and then Old Virgil asked, "Where have you been so early in the morning?"

"We've been calling on Henry and his new wife."

The old man looked up at us with a sudden glitter of malice in his eyes.

"How'd you like her?" he asked.

"All right!" said grandad. "I think she'll make him a good wife."

"Looks to me like a chippy and Emma Kleinfelter heared in town that she was a Polack too."

"Well, I suppose she is different from the women around here. But maybe it's a good idea that Henry went outside for a wife. Just about everybody is related to everybody else here in the Valley."

Old Virgil chuckled and it was a wicked sound. Standing there looking up at us, gnarled and hardbitten, he looked like an evil gnome. Everybody called him "Old Virgil," but he wasn't really old. I suppose he wasn't fifty yet but he looked sixty-five or more. He was always having hard luck or people were always cheating him on a deal. He didn't speak to half the people in the Valley.

Now Virgil asked, "Are you in a hurry?" And grandad said "No, not particularly."

My grandfather had helped him many times with small loans when the banks would have none of him or in advice on the innumerable and interminable lawsuits which seemed somehow to give him satisfaction and recompense. It always astonished me that my grandfather took any trouble about him for I knew how much he disliked Virgil. The only clue I ever had was when I heard him say one night to Aunt Susan, "Well, someone has to lend a hand to wretched people like Old Virgil. I can afford to do so. His neighbors can't. They can't in more ways than one."

Old Virgil now asked, "Well, what about stoppin' for a minute to talk to Mattie? She's been more poorly than usual lately and when she's poorly she's cantankerous. A visit from you would brighten her up."

My grandfather hesitated, I knew too what he felt about Mattie, Old Virgil's wife, for I had heard him discuss her at supper with Aunt Susan. Then his better nature won and he said, "All right! If you'll tie up Ben." Then he turned to me and said, "Come along, Ronnie. I'm sure Mattie'll want to see you."

"That's right," said Old Virgil, "she never gets out. It'll help a lot to cheer her up."

Old Virgil tied Ben to the hitching rail, and my grandfather and I walked slowly up the worn brick path through the ragged garden. The lawn and the flower garden were, of course, a woman's business and Mattie had been "poorly" for over twenty years. But the house wasn't much better. It had not seen paint for a good many years and the metal eaves trough hung loose across the front.

Old Virgil, scuttling along rather like a crab, caught up with us and led the way up the worn steps and opened the front door which in the fashion of the Pennsylvania Dutch from whom Virgil was descended, opened directly into the general living-room. The shades were drawn and although the room was untidy, you had the impression that it was never used and that Virgil spent all his time in the kitchen. There was a faint, unpleasant, sweetish smell in the room which grew suddenly intense and sickening as Virgil opened the door into the room where the invalid lay. It was a mingled smell of red flannel and medicines and kerosene with a hint of nastier things. The room was quite dark save for narrow cracks of light that came from the edges of the window shades. In a corner, although the day was warm, an old-fashioned kerosene stove was burning.

44

In an abnormally loud voice Old Virgil said, "I've brought you company, Mattie. It's the Judge and his grandson, Ronnie." And from the shadows came a voice that was less a voice than a whine. It said, "How do you do, Judge? Virgil, pull up the shade so I can see them."

Old Virgil raised the window shade a little way and the woman in the bed pushed herself up on her thin elbows. As my eyes grew accustomed to the dimness, I could see the pinched face, chalky, transparent white, the color of insects I had seen in the big caves or in the rotten logs which were unaccustomed to the light and which scurried to dark corners the moment light touched them.

"Well, Mattie," said grandad, "how are you?"

The whine answered him. "Just about the same. Doc White has just about given me up."

"What does he think it is?"

Old Virgil answered with a kind of pride, "Says he's never seen anything like it! It's got him baffled!" He sighed and added, as if the woman were not there at all. "It's pretty hard on a man to have a wife who's no good."

The voice from the bed answered, "It's harder on me than on you, Virgil. God knows, I wish I had my strength back."

Then the three of them began to gossip and Virgil's wife wanted to know all about the woman Henry had brought back from the World's Fair.

"I must say," she whined, "it's a funny thing to do —go off to St. Louis for a woman with all the pretty, healthy girls that live right here in the Valley."

Mattie got no further for the door opened and there entered the room a big girl of about sixteen years old. She was plump to the point of fatness with a great moon-face which even in the dim light you could see was high-colored and rather stupid, a little like a pig-face but without the shrewd intelligence which shines out so brightly from the tiny eyes of a pig.

She was carrying a tray with a cup and a tea pot on it and she said to Mattie, "Here's your pennyroyal, Missus."

The smell of the hot pennyroyal tea came into the room but it had none of the mintlike freshness of the pennyroyal which filled all the warm, clean air of the woods pastures when you trod it underfoot on a hot day. The herblike cleanness of the smell was somehow corrupted by the other smells of the overheated, darkened room.

The big, overgrown girl put the tray on a table beside the bed and went out and before she had even left the room, Old Virgil, with a sly look at my grandfather said, "That's Al Kleinfelter's girl, Emma. She's been helpin' out for six months now." And then almost immediately added, "It's a hardship for a man not to have children of his own . . .

to have to send out and pay money to a neighbor for the things he ought to have by his own right."

I listened, half-disinterested, half-disturbed. The smell of medicine, kerosene, red flannel and corrupted pennyroyal grew more and more overpowering and I felt that I was going to be sick. I said, "May I go and look at the pigs?"

"Yes," my grandfather said, "But don't go too far away. I'm going in a few minutes."

I went out of the depressing house just in time and was sick in the ragged lilac bushes. It was not only the smell of the place that was unendurable; it was something else, which was worse than the smell, something I did not understand at all which frightened me.

Presently my grandfather came out and we were on our way home. I asked, "What is wrong with Old Virgil's wife?"

"I don't know. I don't think anybody knows, not even Mattie herself."

"How long has she been like that?"

"It's more than twenty years since she took to her bed." He added, "Sometimes, Ronnie, people just get sick of life, especially if they don't have any resources."

I didn't quite understand what he meant and this he divined. He said, "You see, people like Mattie and Virgil live in a very narrow world—just a pigeonhole in a universe that's full of so

47

many things that a man couldn't begin to understand or enjoy them all if he lived to be a million years old. You see, people like that don't see what's right under their noses. Sometimes it's not their fault but mostly it is. Mattie and Virgil never had much of an education. That might have helped but sometimes people who have educations are just like them."

He was silent for a moment and then went on, "They just turn in on themselves. They aren't very happy people. It's a bad thing to shut yourself off from life. Always remember that, son. Don't turn your back on things. You can never know too much. You can never do all the things there are to do, no matter how long you live. If you're interested in the universe, then the painful things that happen to you aren't so important or so painful."

He touched Old Ben gently with the whip and the old stallion showed a sudden fire again. Then the old man said, "I doubt if you'll find a happier woman than your Aunt Susan. She'd never take to her bed like Mattie."

I listened, thinking that maybe for the first time something painful had happened to me when Henry took a wife and suddenly removed himself from my world and my age. I'd have to find something interesting to take the place of what I'd lost. It was my discovery of how pain could come of affection and human relations, even from someone like Henry who would, I knew, never dream of hurting me.

As if answering my thoughts the old man said, "It's a good idea not to be too possessive with people."

I didn't know then how much he had meant by all he had said. I didn't know then that, in a way, he had been talking to himself all the time and not to me at all.

When we arrived home, we found that Aunt Susan had gone off unexpectedly to town and left word that she wouldn't be home until late, after she'd called on Henry and his new wife.

Grandad said, "Sure as anything she's gone to buy a wedding gift."

That night at supper the talk between grandad and Aunt Susan was mostly about Henry's new wife, Vinnie. Apparently Aunt Susan's call had been partly a success, partly a failure.

Vinnie was dressed up awaiting Aunt Susan. The dressed-up clothes were not country dressed-up clothes but the city kind. The leg-of-mutton sleeves were too large and the cut of the skirt exaggerated and impractical even for "dressed-up" clothes in the country, and Vinnie wore a good deal of cheap jewelry.

"She's not very talkative," said grandad.

To which Aunt Susan replied, "She's shy. Don't forget she's come to a strange new country where she doesn't know anyone. She doesn't understand our ways. And she's got a foreign background."

"Old Virgil says she is Polish."

"It could be," said Aunt Susan, "with her blue eyes and broad high cheekbones and she's got the sturdy build of a peasant."

"Why didn't you ask her?"

Aunt Susan's voice showed a little irritation. "You can't go that fast," she said. "She didn't volunteer any information regarding her background, so I didn't ask. There is such a thing, Tom, as delicacy."

At first it seemed that Vinnie behaved just as she had done with us, sitting there on the cool verandah above the springhouse, answering "yes" and "no."

Aunt Susan said, "It was only when I got to talking about manure and rotations that she began to show signs of life. A bright look came into her eyes and she told me about how her mother had had trouble with her orchard until she turned the whole orchard into a chicken run. And after that the trees bore and the fruit was better and she didn't have any more trouble with insects. That's the only hint she gave of her background but she must have come off a farm. She talked about

Henry's place. She said it was nice and good land and that he had some fine cows."

Then Aunt Susan seemed to lose herself for a moment in thought while Jackson passed the dessert. Presently she said, "I told her about my birds and said I'd send her over the two books and she seemed to like that." Again she reflected for a moment and then said, "I must say she's a fine looking woman. I'd like to see her in country clothes. She isn't the type to be dressed up the way she was this afternoon. She isn't pretty. She's more than that. Sometimes she seems ugly and sometimes beautiful. It's that changeable kind of beauty which is the greatest beauty of all."

Until that moment I hadn't thought of her as really beautiful at all but now I saw what Aunt Susan meant. The beauty flashed out when she smiled, even when the smile was a shy, timid smile, a smile which seemed touched by pain. It was there all the time, just beneath the surface.

Then almost at once Aunt Susan said, "The girl struck me as having been hurt or frightened by something. The thing I can't make out is how Henry ever met up with her."

My grandfather chuckled, "You'll find out soon enough and Henry won't even know that he's told you. But when you do find out I want to know too."

"I think Henry's found himself a good wife and I think he's in love with her. You could see the change in him when he came up to join us before milking. It's a good thing he's married. He was pretty restless and he needed a woman to look after him. It's going to be difficult for them here in the Valley, and we've got to do all we can to help them."

"Of course," said my grandfather. "Henry's like a son to me."

Then as a kind of afterthought Aunt Susan said, "I only hope she won't go out much until the dye has gone out of her hair."

In a kind of illumination I understood all the things that Aunt Susan had not said. I understood that the dyed hair was a sign of a chippy and that in spite of everything my grandfather had said, Vinnie had been a chippy and that they both knew it. I knew too that they wanted desperately for Henry to be happy and that both of them were afraid.

Then grandad said, "We paid a visit to Mattie this morning and she said she'd like to see you."

"I can't stand that smelly room," said Aunt Susan tartly, "and I can't stand Mattie."

The memory of the awful smell of the invalid's room returned to me, corroding the whole room and even the taste of the fresh strawberries.

A twinkle came into my grandfather's eye, "That's not a very charitable way to talk of an unfortunate invalid."

"Unfortunate! Rubbish! There's nothing the matter with Mattie. She took to her bed to get away from Virgil's touching her. You remember that just before she took sick she and Virgil lived in the same house without speaking to each other. She didn't have the courage to walk out on him or the brains to figure out any better way of getting away from him but to take to her bed in that awful, smelly room. He's a mean, penurious old horror and Mattie's a whining weakling and a fool. If she's really sick it's only because she's made herself sick living for twenty years and more in that evil-smelling room. And now Virgil's got that half-witted Kleinfelter girl in the house with him on the pretense that he needs her to look after Mattie. It's an evil business and some day something terrible is going to happen there. Sometimes when I hear people talk about the beauty of country life and the simplicity of country people, I think they're fools or crazy. If they only knew sometimes the things that go on in the country. It makes me sick even to step inside the door of Mattie's house!"

Then quite suddenly the indignation seemed to fade out and in the flat voice of duty, she added, "But I'll stop in and see her. Maybe she can't help being what she is."

After supper my grandfather and I went out to the stable to see a new foal.

53

As the day wore on, it had grown steadily warmer as it often did in that part of the country and by eight in the evening the atmosphere was really hot and muggy with the haze of heat laying over the whole Valley. The air was very still as if the whole of the universe was paused awaiting a calamity.

We did not return to the house until the sun had slipped out of sight behind the great black clouds that had begun to pile up in the west. The stillness persisted. It was so still that even the leaves on the trees showed no movement but hung lifeless and fixed, like the leaves of trees in a picture. And then, as we returned to the house and crossed the recently clipped lawn between the iron deer and the ornate flower beds, there came up suddenly out of nowhere a violent wind and there was the sound of doors and windows being closed rapidly as Jackson and Aunt Susan hurried from room to room to shut out the oncoming storm.

I went up to my room and lighted the lamp and then almost immediately put it out again, and in the darkness went to the window to watch the storm over the Valley. The wind was really blowing now, bending the young trees along the lane almost to the ground. There was the sound of a great roar as it swept down the Valley and now and then there came a quick and brilliant flash of lightning that illumined the whole of the beaten landscape with a cold blue clarity that was brighter than daylight. And the brilliant light was followed by wild claps of thunder. At times for a second or two you could see all the way as far as Henry's farm and the Wild Country and the big lake.

Storms had never frightened me even as a small child and when the rains began to fall in great torrents of water, I now felt a sudden relief and actual pleasure. And while I sat there watching the storm and trying to fathom all the intimations of the conversation I had heard at supper and understand all the things which had not been said, I think I began to discern a little the fashion in which human lives become interwoven into patterns which moved toward inevitable ends. I was still a child and confused by the half-revelations of the conversation between two old people whose knowledge and experience and wisdom permitted them to converse with each other only in fragments and hints and intimations. And I was aware of a great desire to grow up quickly, to become a man and bring home a woman as Henry had done, so that I could understand all the things which the others knew so well that they had no real reason to explain them to each other. Henry had moved now into the realm of grown-ups, leaving me behind alone in the realm of children, which grown-ups forget so easily, seeing only its brightness and forgetting its peculiar half-animal misery and confusion and jealousies. I thought that if I grew up quickly and went out and brought home a woman as Henry had done, everything might be the same between us again.

The quick storm died away presently and I went to bed in the darkness to sleep without moving until I heard the big bell beside the kitchen door ringing for breakfast.

June slid imperceptibly into the heat of July and with the heat there came a dullness into my heart and into everything I did. For the first time the big stock farm and the Wild Country in the lower Valley lost its excitement and its beauty. I went swimming and fishing with the other farm kids and joined in the horse-shoe pitching and one-old-cat games of the white and colored boys about the stables, but there was a singular dullness about everything. Only at moments did I experience any of the old satisfaction or that sense of every day being too short to encompass all the potential delights of that particular life and landscape.

Once in the cool, dark, inside hallway I heard Aunt Susan say to my grandfather, "What's the matter with Ronnie? He doesn't seem to have any spirit about anything. Maybe we'd better take him to Doctor Lee and have him gone over."

And I heard my grandfather say, "It isn't anything, Susan. It's just his age. At that age things begin to happen to boys. Girls get silly and giggle and boys begin to change from children into men. It's a tough process they go through. It makes them do all kinds of wild and foolish things. He'll come out of it. Don't worry."

What I overheard disturbed me, but it comforted me too, since it explained what was happening to me and the unmistakable signs I couldn't help observing which indicated that I was beginning to change and to grow into a man.

You see, I was in a peculiar position, with no father or mother. There was only myself, a child of thirteen and then a great gap and then my grandfather who was seventy-three and Aunt Susan who was so bird-like and virginal. Between them and me there was no one with whom I could talk of any of these things—except Henry. We had never talked of such things in the past because Henry was himself, I think, almost as innocent as I was, and he had that simplicity of mind which did not brood, nor have strange, complicated perverse thoughts. And he was, until he encountered Vinnie, totally without experience in love.

It wasn't that I didn't know the facts of life. One couldn't live on a farm or around a breeding stable without knowing them, either from the animals or from the rough conversation of the men and boys. I had always known and I had accepted these facts as far back as I could remember. What troubled me was the fashion in which they affected people. With livestock, everything was simple and uncomplicated, but the facts of life did strange things to people. There was Henry and Vinnie, and the strange business of Old Virgil and Mattie and the half-witted Kleinfelter girl and I suspected that the facts of life were involved in the story of the mysterious "Melissa" my grandfather and Aunt Susan were always talking about. And there was always the usual country gossip and the hasty marriages and all the rest.

I knew that my grandfather was partly right about what was wrong with me, although I knew, but vaguely that he had not hit upon the whole of the reason. There was Henry for whom I had not only a sort of hero worship but with whom, I know now, I was in a way in love as a schoolgirl gets a "crush" upon a teacher or a boy for some athletic hero. I was at that age when I was neither child nor man, when in my universe Henry seemed the most desirable creature I had ever known. I even dreamed of him at night. There was nothing sordid or perverse in the feeling. It was simply that I wanted to be *like* Henry. I wanted to *become* Henry, to *be* Henry, with his strong handsome young body and his capacity for doing all the things from swimming to plowing to riding a horse better than anyone I had ever known. But I did not understand these things. I only knew that I was hurt because Vinnie had come between me and Henry and because I could no longer wander down the Valley with Prince and help Henry with the chores or go fishing or swimming with him or sleep in the great double bed beside him when I spent the night at his farm.

For nearly a month I did not see him at all for he was busy with haymaking and oats and wheat harvest and he had added six more cows to his dairy herd which took extra time and work. In the old days none of that would have made any difference for I could only have been a help to him. I would have gone over and worked in the fields, driving the big horses which drew the haywagons. But now there was Vinnie and they were newly married and my grandfather had hinted strongly that they did not want a thirteen-year-old boy hanging around. I had enough sophistication to understand that.

To my grandfather it did not seem strange that I no longer went off for the night to Henry's farm or strange that Henry no longer dropped in after chores were finished in the evening. He accepted that fact as a person of his age would inevitably do. It never occurred to him that the change could cause suffering in the heart of an adolescent boy, perhaps as much suffering as I was ever to experience in a long life, for a child's suffering can be very real and very deep and all the worse since a child has neither the wisdom nor the resources of mature men and women. His misery fills the whole of his world, leaving no space for other things. He has only emotions with no reason, with no cynicism or resignation to dull the edges of his jealousy or suffering. Those people who think of adolescence as a happy, carefree time either possess deficient emotions or inadequate memories.

And then one evening I saw Henry's buckboard coming up the long township road which crossed the Valley. He was driving it and he was alone, and suddenly the whole of that small world became bright again, illumined by my own dazzling, all-enveloping happiness. As much as any woman awaiting the arrival of her lover, I was swept by impatience and emotion. It seemed that the buckboard took hours to cross the wide fertile Valley. I debated whether I should leave the verandah and run down the lane to meet him or whether I should stay on the steps and pretend not to notice his approach until he had arrived. What was a simple visit became a tumultuous, complex and momentous affair. Three months earlier I would have run quite naturally down to the gate. Now for some reason I could not.

But at last I could bear it no longer and went down the path between the ornate deer and flower beds and was waiting for him by the horse block

—a little, cast-iron painted Negro stableboy—
when he drove up. I felt that if he had not turned
in at the driveway under the arch marked "Clarendon Stock Farm," I would have died. He turned
in and presently he was there and I took the tie-
strap of his horse and fastened it into the ring
held in the hand of the little cast-iron stableboy.

He jumped down and said, "Hello, Ronnie!"
He was dressed in store clothes and a necktie
which made him look awkward and countrified
since they never fit him physically or spiritually.
He only looked himself in old country clothes
which seemed at once to take on the shape of his
figure. He wore no hat and in the heat the black
curls fell over his forehead. At sight of him I felt
a sudden surge of happiness and fulfillment and
then a quick disappointment for his "Hello, Ronnie!" was casual, the greeting of a mature man to
a small boy, with none of the old, warm feeling in
it of comradeship and equality.

He said, "I haven't seen any of you folks for a
long time. I just thought I'd drive over and say
'hello.' Is your grandfather at home?"

I told him "yes" and felt hurt that it was my
grandfather he had come over to see and not me.

As we went up the path, side by side, he put his
arm about my shoulder and said, "I haven't seen
you for a long time. Where have you been?"

I just said that I didn't know why I hadn't been over. I guessed I was just too busy.

"Well, I've missed you," said Henry.

Then my grandfather came out of the house and I saw his face light up with pleasure at the sight of Henry and knew that in his own way he felt as I did—only he was at the other end of life when you could no longer be hurt, or so I thought.

We sat down in the big rockers and Jackson brought us lemonade, for Henry in his innocence and in the tradition of the Valley people did not even drink beer. He had never tasted the juleps that were commonplace at the Big House.

While I sat, quiet, happy, admiring the two men, they talked Valley-talk of the weather and the crops. Henry said he had been too busy with harvest to leave his farm. Vinnie, he said, was a great help. She could handle a team in the field as well as any man. He didn't like to have his wife working in the fields but Vinnie seemed to like it, even better than housework—not that she neglected her housekeeping—the house was kept as well as it had been kept when his mother was alive. Indeed, it was, he was afraid he'd have to say, kept even better. Vinnie was always washing, scouring and scrubbing.

I listened, jealous and envious, and then quite suddenly I was happy again when I heard Henry say, "I just drove over to see if you'd let Ronnie come over and spend a couple of days. It's been a long time since he's spent a night at the farm."

So that was why he had come. Everything was suddenly all right again, especially when I heard my grandfather say, "Of course, I think it would do Ronnie good."

I rushed in quickly, saying, "Shall I go and pack now?" But my grandfather was less headlong. He said, "There's not that much hurry. I'll drive you over tomorrow morning, early."

Well, that was better than nothing.

Then the three of us went out to see the four or five new foals that had been born since Henry had last been at Clarendon Farm. I am afraid I swaggered a little and talked big about bone and hock and withers. I was trying to be a grown man and their equal. And suddenly I saw by the twinkle in my grandfather's eye that he understood what I was doing.

In the morning, early, before the heat had come up, Old Ben was brought around and harnessed to the dogcart.

In a month the whole appearance of the Valley had changed. The lush green hay was cut and the wheat fields, where the wheat had not already been cut and shocked, were golden brown, rippling in the fresh breeze of the early morning.

As we came out of the woods by Old Virgil's

farm, we saw a horse and sulky standing by the mailbox with a man seated in the sulky. He held his straw hat in his hands and the shock of red hair told us who he was. The big, half-witted Kleinfelter girl was standing by the mailbox talking to him. As we drove past my grandfather said, "Good morning, Emma. Hello, Red," but did not stop. He did not stop, but I saw his face darken and I knew he was disturbed.

"Red" was Red McGovern. He was my grandfather's trainer and his best driver in the trotting-races on the Grand Circuit, a small, tough man of thirty or thirty-five who had been born in North Ireland and was wonderful with horses. As my grandfather often said in talking with other horse owners, "Red is worth his weight in gold. When he gets behind a horse he becomes a horse himself."

You could understand what my grandfather meant. Red had driven more winners in his day than any other driver on the Circuit. And he actually was like a horse—like a small and fiery stallion. He had a small, wiry body, well-muscled and compact, with very bright blue eyes, a mop of red hair and a hard, sensual mouth. He wasn't good-looking, for his face had a slight resemblance to the face of a weasel but there was something about him—perhaps simply the vitality and the force and warmth of a man who is forever pursuing women

—which gave him great success as a lady-killer. He was the dirtiest talker around the stables and was forever telling, in considerable detail, the conquests he had made. He walked with a swagger and an assurance which made him unpopular with other men and many times my grandfather had had to get him out of scrapes, with women or because of some dubious tactic at the tracks. Yet when he was handling a horse his whole manner and even his appearance seemed to change. The hardness about the mouth vanished and a warmth came into his voice. It may have been, of course, that the same change came over him when he touched a woman, and so explained not only his temporary success but the fact that he was never able to rid himself of them once he became bored or satiated. That, of course, we could never know.

There was a feeling of ruthlessness and hardness about him which made me avoid him, and I did not like the way he talked about women, as if they existed only for his own sensual pleasure. I knew, too, that my grandfather disliked him for I had heard him again and again discuss Red with my Aunt Susan. He would say, "Sometimes I don't think it's worth it, keeping Red. He's in trouble again. But I can't do without him. There isn't another man in the business as good with horses. I never need worry about them whether I'm there or not."

And now as my grandfather's face grew dark and he kept silent nearly all the way to Henry's place, I knew he didn't like what he had seen— Red "monkeying around" the Kleinfelter girl. The cold greeting—indeed the whole encounter—had been completely insignificant, but the change in my grandfather's manner made it somehow important and menacing.

When we arrived at Henry's farm there was nobody at the house and we drove down the long lane to Henry's far fields which lay beyond the woods. There in a wheat field freshly cut with the sheaves neatly stacked, we found Henry and Vinnie.

In the heat Henry had taken off his shirt and was stripped to the waist, pitching the sheaves high onto a wagon drawn by his team of big Percheron mares. The sweat streamed down his body, and under the tanned skin the muscles moved and flowed with his effort like the muscles beneath the skin of a panther. High up on the wagon, a pitchfork in her hand, stood Vinnie, balancing herself with a curious wild grace when she picked up the reins and drove the team from shock to shock of sheaves. She wore a short calico dress with very little underneath it and I saw for the first time how strong she was and how beautiful a body she had. Her hair she wore in braids wrapped around her head. The yellow dye was disappearing. Her skin was no longer a pallid white but had that light golden tan which the skin of northern blond people takes on when exposed to strong summer sunlight.

They didn't see us until we were almost upon them, as Vinnie pulled up the team and turned to pick up her fork, and they were suddenly embarrassed, as if we had come upon them in some sudden act of intimacy. Vinnie knelt down on the high piled sheaves and Henry, after greeting us, called up to Vinnie to throw down his shirt which he put on at once.

"I didn't expect you so early or Vinnie and I would have had more clothes on." But my grandfather only laughed and said, "Why dress up to go harvesting on a hot day? Don't be a fool, Henry! Take your shirt off."

Henry obeyed him and said with the odd pride of a Valley farmer, "I was going to get a man to help but Vinnie wouldn't let me. She said what was the use wasting money when she liked to load wheat." Then he looked up at her with the shining look of a young man who was body and soul in love with a woman—one woman to the exclusion of all else in the world. And she smiled down at him with the look of a mother who is proud of her child.

She said, "Sure! I enjoy it. It ain't heavy work." The faint accent was in her words. She almost said "enchoy" for "enjoy" but the agonizing shyness which had marred our first visit was gone out of her, perhaps because she belonged here under the sky in the sun in the midst of the harvest.

Then Henry told me to climb up on the wagon and help Vinnie with building the load and my grandfather stayed until the full load was built, and then he and Old Ben led the way back to the big barns and bade us good-bye saying he'd come back for me day after tomorrow evening.

In the mow I helped Henry stack the sheaves. Vinnie pitched them to us off the wagon. It was hot, dusty work, but it didn't matter. I was happy again there in the mow working with Henry. And Vinnie didn't seem to come between us now. Suddenly she seemed more like a man, a good friend of ours. The three of us were comrades.

We brought sheaves into the barn all the rest of the day and knocked off at five o'clock to do the chores. Then Vinnie looked at me and said, "Maybe you'd like to help Henry with the milking and feeding the calves. I got plenty to do in the house." And for the first time there was understanding between us. In an odd way I divined that she understood everything and wanted to make me happy.

I took Henry's collie, Rex, and set out with him down across the lower pasture, walking barefoot through the bluegrass and mint and white clover to the spot where the cows lay by the edge of the creek beneath the great willows. Rex could have done the job alone at a word of command from me, but in my happiness I wanted to savor to the full the whole of the experience, and the warm grass and the scent of the mint crushed under foot was a part of it.

Henry let me milk the quieter of the cows—old Dora and Spot—who didn't mind amateur bungling. I turned the handle of the separator and helped Henry carry the warm, foaming skim milk down to the trough where the bright, intelligent-eyed hogs came running and squealing at the sight of us, and afterward I took the big buckets of yellow cream down the steps of the big springhouse and poured the cream into big crocks set deep in a stone trough filled with icy cold water alongside the big crocks of yellow butter and buttermilk. These were all the things I had once done until Vinnie came and now Vinnie let me do them.

There was a wonderful supper—not just a country supper—but something special which I knew had been concocted by Vinnie because there was company, because a friend of Henry's had come to visit. There was a rich vegetable soup, better than I have ever tasted since, and cold fried chicken which she must have made the night before after she came in from the fields, and new peas fresh out of the garden she had made and kept herself behind the house, and new lettuce with sugar and vinegar dressing and a big lemon pie and coffee more fragrant than any coffee has ever seemed to me before or since. It was not at all like the bachelor snacks Henry and I had concocted, mostly out of cans, in the days after his mother died. You could see that Henry appreciated the difference. He kept grinning and looking at me when I took a second piece of chicken and then a third.

Once he said, "Vinnie's a good cook, ain't she, Ronnie?" And turning to her, he said, "It's better than we used to have . . . Ronnie and me."

And after supper Vinnie said, "Why don't you boys go for a swim while I wash up?"

That was the pinnacle of delight for the whole day and it was Vinnie who had thought of it, of something I had not dared hope for. So Henry and I and Rex set out down across the meadow to the big hole in the creek where we had gone swimming together in the past on just such long warm summer evenings.

Among the willows we stripped off our clothes and dived and swam and splashed in the warm air and water and presently lay in the mint and blue-grass watching the moon rise above the wooded hills of the Wild Country. We didn't talk at all except when Henry said once, "Listen to the bobwhite calling. Probably has a nest of young ones somewhere over in the meadow." In the pool where our swimming and diving had disturbed the minnows, they returned now and began jumping out of the water after the insects which floated on the surface. The evening was so still that the faintest splash made by the tiniest silver fish was audible.

I was happy again, happier I think than I have ever been before or since, for I came very close to that wonderfully beautiful and simple and innocent and natural world in which Henry lived all of his life—a world which I would never have known save perhaps through him, when for a moment I was permitted to feel it quite close to me, intangible and real, yet forbidden to me alone by the very complexity of my own nature which was aware of too much.

Finally, when the moon was well up and the air had begun to turn cool and our naked bodies had dried, we put on our clothes and started back across the pasture. As we drew near the old white house, the sound of music came toward us, faint at first, as faint as the scent of the mint crushed beneath our bare feet, and then slowly clearer and more distinct. It was gay music with a tingling rhythm which invited the feet to dancing and made the heart light, music such as one rarely heard in the Valley. There was a richness in it and a wild rhythm one never heard in the music at our square dances which was thin music.

Henry said, "It's Vinnie. She's awfully good on the accordion." And we walked a little faster to return to her.

She was seated in a rocker on the big porch with an accordion on her knees. It was a big, shiny instrument bright with metal and ivory and as she played she swayed to the rhythm as if she were dancing. She did not stop playing as we came up in the moonlight but finished the piece.

Then she said, "That was a Polish dance like my parents used to dance in the old country."

Henry said, "Sing us something." But she turned shy. "I don't know any English words and if I sing in Polish, Ronnie wouldn't understand what it was about."

It was easy to see that she was ashamed of being "foreign." But Henry persuaded her, and she said, "I'll sing just one in Polish. It's a story about a young village girl who loved a neighbor boy. She was pretty and he was young and handsome and they loved each other but there come to their village a rich and handsome stranger who made love to the young girl and she fell in love with him and forgot her young peasant lover and then one night the peasant lover met the stranger outside the house of the girl and they fought with daggers and hurt each other so both of them died. And the girl never married anybody and didn't have no children and grandchildren but just lived alone until she was an old woman. She sings the song when she was an old woman." She sighed and then added, "It is a sad sonk!"

She played a few bars on the accordion and then began to sing in a deep warm voice of great beauty. It was not a trained voice but it was young and fresh and she sang naturally as a thrush sings in a hedgerow. The language, of which neither Henry nor I understood a word, seemed wild and beautiful and very strange there in the Valley.

It was a happy evening, but after I had gone to bed, the jealousy returned to me as I lay awake in the big walnut bed in the "spare room." I had begun to like Vinnie. She made everything so warm and so easy. It was as if she considered Henry and me of the same age, as if she had set out to mother us both. But now that night had come, the relationship between her and Henry had returned, shutting me out. In the old days when I stayed overnight at Henry's farm, we had shared the same room and even the same bed in order to save laundry, and now Vinnie was there in my place.

I lay very still, listening, but in the solidly built old house sounds did not travel easily and I heard nothing save the croaking of the frogs and now and then the hoot of an owl or the distant barking

73

of a fox in the brilliant moonlight. I did not know what I was listening for; it was certainly not from any perverse or obscene reason. I was caught up in a mixture of innocence and loneliness and curiosity, wondering what it was that went on between a man and woman in love with each other, what it was that I should have to wait for a long time to discover, what it was that had made Henry suddenly a man, setting him apart from me. I wondered how they had come to meet and what it was that made them know they were in love, what it was that had compelled Henry to ask Vinnie to marry him and come home with him to his bed for the rest of his life. . . . What it was that brought the shining look into his dark eyes whenever he looked at her.

I think I have never been so lonely as I was on that moonlit night. The melody of the song Vinnie had sung to us about the girl in some distant, mythical Polish village, kept returning to me, in fragments, haunting me, and then quite suddenly the weariness of the long day and the strain on the muscles of a healthy, growing boy, overcame me and I fell asleep.

PART II

THE ANNUAL CHURCH SUPPER ALWAYS FELL IN
August. It was held to raise funds for repairs and
painting and nearly everyone in the whole Valley
turned up. Even the oldest men and women, some
of them barely able any longer to totter from the
buggy to the long tables laid under the trees, came
to the annual supper to exchange gossip and see
neighbors whom they rarely encountered during
the rest of the year.

The day before at supper, Aunt Susan said, "I
think this would be a good time for Vinnie to meet
the other people of the Valley."

My grandfather who had been thinking of other
things, looked up suddenly and said, "Why?
Haven't they called on her?"

"No. I'm afraid they haven't."

"Why?"

"I think it's mostly Old Virgil's work. He's
spread that story up and down the whole Valley.
The old fool has worked at it. Only old Mrs.

75

Herschell has called and she only went so she could gossip."

"It doesn't seem possible," said grandad.

"There's a lot of venom in it. Old Virgil hates her and Henry too because they've got what he's never had and never will have. All he's ever had is Mattie and that half-witted Kleinfelter girl."

"Susan!" said grandad and laughed. "You're as bad as old Mrs. Herschell."

"Well, it's true," said Aunt Susan.

Then there was silence and presently my grandfather said, "Maybe they won't be nice to her."

Aunt Susan raised her head and a glittery look, like the look in the eye of an angry bluejay, came into the gentle grey eyes. "They'd better be nice to her," she said, "or they'll hear some things that haven't been well-aired since the Valley was settled. I haven't lived here off and on all my life without learning a lot. Besides," she added, "I was going to drive them over myself in the surrey. You and Ronnie can go in the dogcart." Then she went into the bird-like language which suited her so well. "I'll keep both of them under my wing all evening." And I found myself chuckling inwardly at the picture of Aunt Susan as a tiny bird, trying to keep Henry and Vinnie under her wings like a hedge sparrow with young that have long outgrown the nest.

"Just leave it to me," she said, and then after a moment, "The dye has about gone out of her hair and she's got some country clothes. She doesn't look any different from anybody else in the Valley."

After supper, grandad and I walked out to the stables. He seemed silent and troubled and didn't take his usual interest in the horses although we walked from stall to stall and paddock to paddock looking at them all. It was a lovely soft evening with the night coming down blue and slow, and from the row of houses beyond the stables where the Negro stableboys and their families lived came the sound of singing. One of the boys was playing a concertina and another a banjo and two high-yaller girls were shuffling improvised dance steps on the dusty earth. We came up quietly and unobserved and my grandfather, rather than interfere with the music and fun, stopped by the paddock fence and lifted his long, lean body upward to seat himself on the top rail. I imitated him and for a long time we sat there and it seemed to me that the anxiety slowly flowed out of my grandfather. His lean body relaxed and suddenly the old, tired face was smiling at the carefree happiness of the Negroes and the wild rhythm of the music and the dancing.

Then the music stopped and one of the Negro boys turned and saw my grandfather and said, "Why, there's the Judge! Howdy Judge?" And something happened to the little party going on by the cabin door. The gaiety seemed to die. There was a silence broken only by the giggles of one of the high-yaller girls.

Grandad said, "Howdy, Jasper?" And then, "Go on playing. Don't pay any attention to us." But Jasper didn't obey him and the curious silence broken by the whispering and giggling persisted. Then my grandfather said, "Have you seen Mister Red about?" And Jasper answered, "He ain't here. He went out early."

The Negro laughed, "All dressed up fit to kill in his plaid shirt like he was goin' courtin' again."

"All right! Thanks Jasper. Go on with your party. We'll be moving along." But suddenly there was an overtone of weariness in his voice.

We slipped down from the fence and started away toward the harvest moon which had begun to rise large and golden as a great pumpkin far down the Valley over the Wild Country. As we turned out of sight around the corner of the stables, the music began again.

My grandfather said, "It's a pity. We spoiled their fun." And like a small child, I asked, "Why?"

"I wish I could tell you, son. They're a happy people when they're among themselves. We just can't enter into it."

Then as we walked he was silent for a time and presently as if he had been thinking he said, "Maybe someday we can—when the world's a better place. There's so much that people have to

78

learn and understand." He put his lean arm about my shoulder. "But don't worry about it, son . . . at least not yet. You'll have time to worry later on . . . plenty of it."

Then he said suddenly, "Wayne Torrance is coming on Thursday." And I felt my spirits rise. That was good news. Wayne was always full of high spirits and he always brought presents with him for all of us. Suddenly I was a small boy again, thinking of Wayne only as someone whose presence seemed to quicken the pace of everything at Clarendon.

"Is he going to stay long?" I asked.

"No. Only till Saturday. He's a busy man now . . . important too." There was pride in his voice as he repeated, "Yes . . . he's done very well. He's filled my expectations." It was as if the boy he had helped were his own son.

The light of day was gone now and the moonlight had taken its place with a moon which, risen high now, was no longer big and golden but becoming slowly small and clear like a disk of burnished, shining silver. We reached the house and grandad said, "You'd better go to bed now. It's late. It's a pity the days have already begun to shorten."

I went up to my room, undressed, turned out the light, and crawled into the huge carved walnut double bed, but I did not fall asleep. Much of my

79

daydreaming and indeed much of my thinking happened after I had gone to bed at night in that curious period between wakefulness and sleep when thought seems misted over yet at times unbelievably clear and brilliant. Long ago I had consciously clung to that half-real border world of thought and being, when one is neither asleep nor awake, trying to prolong it until at last I could resist sleep no longer and slid quietly out of the world of reality into a sleep that was like death.

On that particular night I was kept awake longer than usual by the brilliance of the moonlight and by the excitement of anticipation because Wayne Torrance was coming to visit us the day after tomorrow.

When Wayne came to Clarendon Farm something happened. My grandfather and Aunt Susan seemed to brighten up. There was a good deal of laughter and the meals became gayer. The whole tempo of existence was quickened. Wayne was always full of stories about St. Louis, about Washington, about politics. He smoked big and expensive cigars and carried the faint, clean smell of eau-de-cologne.

As I told you earlier, he was a country boy, the son of a farmer over the ridge in Chicopee Valley, whom my grandfather had educated and finally taken into his law firm. At that time of his approaching visit he must have been about thirty-seven years old. He was tall and big, with a very clean complexion, blondish wavy hair. He gave the impression of bigness and force. His hands and feet were big but well-formed and like his face, handsome. His good looks carried with them a great sense of physical well-being and vitality, for he was one of those people who seem to possess inexhaustible energy and high spirits, who feed vitality to others yet who can at the same time, exhaust the spirit. Everything about him seemed a little overdone. He was good-looking, yet his good looks were too big, too florid. His mind, quick and shrewd, was too quick and too shrewd. Everybody liked him down to the littlest pickaninny who learned quickly that his pockets were always filled with candy. He matched story for story with Red McGovern, yet he was equally at home with my grandfather and Aunt Susan upon a plane that was quite different.

His career had been quick and easy. He did well in college and law school, went into my grandfather's law firm and almost at once ran for state legislature and was elected. From then on he had gone ahead until at thirty-two he was the youngest member of Congress. With his good looks and vitality and his "smartness" he could scarcely have failed as a politician. He had the power somehow of quickening the air about him and of charging it with a kind of self-created tension.

My grandfather was proud of him and yet, I think, a little afraid of him as one might be afraid of an uncontrolled and elemental force.

I knew all about this, not through my own wisdom or experience but because I had heard my grandfather and Aunt Susan talk of him hundreds of times. I knew that my grandfather was afraid largely that Wayne might one day do something reckless which might wreck the whole of his brilliant career.

Lying there in the moonlight I thought about him for a long time wondering what he would bring me this time. He always brought some expensive gift and he was very wise about suiting the gift he selected to the number of my increasing years. He never brought a gift that was too old or too young for me. The year before he had brought me a silver-mounted Mexican saddle, a really handsome and expensive gift.

As I lay there, speculating, I could almost smell the fresh aroma of the clean eau-de-cologne and expensive cigars. It would be fun while he was here. He would make grandfather and Aunt Susan laugh and would wander around the stables kidding with the Negro stableboys who worshipped him. The only thing I didn't like were the times when he got together with Red McGovern in the harness room of the stables and they began swapping stories and their experiences with women. At such times they always sent me away, but I knew what they were talking about just the same.

And presently as the path of moonlight shifted and was blotted out completely by the trees, I fell asleep. The last thing of which I was aware was the sound of hoofbeats on the drive. It was Red McGovern returning home in the moonlight from his courting. Sleepily I guessed that it must have been the fat Kleinfelter girl and I remembered the effect upon my grandfather at the sight of them talking beside Old Virgil's mailbox. I saw again for a moment the cloud upon his face and then fell into a deep sleep. But I was aware of a sudden, curious fear—the fear of growing up into a world where everything seemed painful and complex and difficult. Yet to be like Henry, to be able to rejoin him as an equal, I would have to grow up and become a man.

The Valley church was built of red brick with a white painted steeple and stood on the edge of a thick virgin woods which had never been cut off because the hill, rising steeply behind the church, was rough ground filled with the outcroppings of pink sandstone and it was impossible to take out the felled trees. The hillside was honeycombed with caves and littered with huge fragments of stone which in remote times had broken away and slipped down the slope. Long since great trees had grown among the ferns and filled the crevices and cracks of their surface.

Beside the church there was a little graveyard where all the early settlers lay buried. Some of them had been killed in wars with the Indians and some during the Mormon troubles. In a way the whole history of the Valley people could be found there—found there written on the tombstones. My own great-grandfather and great-grandmother lay there under tombstones which told how he had died young and how she had lived to be an old woman.

Each year at the end of the summer, the ladies of the Valley gave a supper to raise funds for repairs and for the heating of the church during the long winter. Accompanied by children of all ages, they began assembling late in the afternoon, coming in buggies and surries from all over the township bearing with them cold chicken, meat loaf, salad, cakes, pies, pickles—all the abundance of that rich, yet half-wild and beautiful country-side. The horses they tied in the long arched shed or to the hitching rail beneath the double row of big Norway spruce. Bridles were taken off and halters substituted and bags of oats emptied into the worn, chewed mangers. Then under the trees long tables were set up, made of boards placed upon trestles, with white tablecloths covering them. If there were still late summer flies about, some of the older children were stationed with fresh-cut branches of maple or oak to drive them away from the rich feast. And as darkness began to fall, the ladies of the church brought out the old-fashioned gasoline flares, hung them against the trees and lighted them. The wavering yellow light cast long black shadows which danced and turned as the flames trembled in the gentle breeze of the evening.

Aunt Susan usually went early to help the ladies but on this occasion she set out a little later to go by and pick up Henry and Vinnie, leaving my grandfather and me to follow. Driving old Ben we started a half hour before sunset and arrived at the Valley church just as the sun was slipping down behind the distant blue and purple hills of the Wild Country. Some of the menfolk had already arrived and my grandfather joined them, leaving me to rush off and find the other boys while he talked of crops and cattle and horses.

The church suppers were great occasions. Most of all perhaps for the small boys for, since the farms of the Valley were widely scattered and there were only one or two small schoolhouses and one traveled only by horse and buggy, they offered great opportunity for all the kids of the Valley to get together, indeed the only opportunity which occurred during the months of summer. Because

I went off to boarding school each autumn and did not return until the following June, I had not even the opportunity of seeing them at school. And beyond the great mountains of food, there were other attractions lying among the great rocks and crevasses of the primeval hillside above the church. Some of the crevasses extended deep underground, opening up sometimes into great underground rooms where there were hidden springs and moisture dripped from the walls and ceilings of the cavern. Some of the openings that formed the entrances were so small that only a small boy could have squeezed his way in. They offered a wonderful playground where the kids could play cops and robbers or hide and seek or could holler to hear the echoes rocketing back and forth. There was added excitement in the legend that once there had been among the trees and the shattered rocks a tremendous battle between the Indians and the settlers and that the spirits of the slaughtered Indians still haunted the place. The boys, out of long custom and habit always brought candle-ends and matches in their pockets.

On Sundays there was never any opportunity to explore the caves because the boys wore their Sunday best and by the time the sermon was over it was time to start on the long drive home to a big Sunday dinner.

There were all sorts of perils involved in these

explorations, real ones as well as the imaginary and fantastic ones. There might be fallen rocks or slides of earth and there was always the peril of rattlesnakes come upon in the dark. And always there was the pungent musky smell of foxes, intensified whenever we crept into some remote corner. In the wavering light of the candles the sight of a dark form slithering away into the darker parts of the cave sent exciting prickles up and down the spine.

That evening the exploration was dull. We came upon no snakes and although we smelled the foxes we never saw any. The fun came out of yelling and showing-off, making horrific sounds which echoed through the hollows of the cavern and trying to squeeze through openings that were too small. We must have played for an hour when the sound of the church bell, summoning us to supper, penetrated the caves with a remote, hollow sound.

Smirched with the dry, sandy dust which covered the floors of the caves, we made our way through one of the openings and suddenly, spread out below us lay the pretty scene of the church supper. Near to us, the newly risen moon cast long black shadows interspersed with clear, silvery light and far down below in the churchyard beneath the black drooping fronds of the ancient spruces, the gasoline flares cast a wavering yellow glow over the laden tables, the farmers in their dark Sunday suits, the bustling women, and the children playing about in bright colored groups.

The other boys, yelling and whooping, raced down the steep slope among the rocks but I found myself lingering behind as if unconsciously to savor the beauty of the scene, as if it were something, a memory perhaps, which I wished to capture and hold for the rest of my life. And there was too a half-conscious reluctance and hesitation as if when I approached the scene it would fall apart into its diverse elements, ugliness and beauty, its meanness and goodness. From where I stood, at a distance, I was safe. Going near, I would lose myself in that web of circumstance and compulsion which drew all those people together sometimes in happiness but more often in what seemed to me to be pain and misery. And so I stood there for a long time among the high virgin trees, detached and lonely, yet strangely happy, until I realized that if I did not descend the slope I would be missed and they would fear some accident had happened to me and would begin to call out or look for me and I would become the humiliated center of interest of all of them.

As I went down the hill I saw that they had begun to sit down at the tables, in friendly little groups. It was only when I came through the gate of the churchyard fence that I noticed Henry and

Vinnie and Aunt Susan were sitting a little apart. My grandfather moved away from the men with whom he had been talking and sat by Vinnie. Aunt Susan was on her other side and then Henry. I went toward them and as I reached the table I saw that Aunt Susan's face was an unnatural red and that her eyes were glittering with a bird-like anger I had never seen in them before. I sat down opposite them a moment after grandad seated himself. I heard him say in a fierce, low voice, "Now, Susie, control yourself!" Then I saw that Vinnie's eyes were moist and I understood what had happened—that someone had been cruel to her. Henry was looking down, his face dark and angry.

My grandfather began to talk, busily, like the diplomat he was. He passed a platter of cold chicken and said, "Henry, there's going to be an early frost this year. You can tell by the moon. It's a cold moon."

Vinnie took a piece of chicken and then suddenly sat very upright. She was dressed now in real country clothes and the dye was almost gone out of her hair. She looked like any other woman at the supper save that she had a proud carriage that was different from the other farm women.

My grandfather kept on talking and I saw that Aunt Susan could not trust herself to speak. She had a quick and fiery tongue which under stress of anger could be cutting and even vicious in its cruelty. I had seen her once turn on Red McGovern when he had struck one of the little Negro boys with a saddle girth. He was a hard man but he quailed before her. When sufficiently provoked she had a terrible way of striking cruelly at the most vulnerable spot. That was what my grandfather was afraid of now—that she might do as she threatened and tell off two or three of the women present. If she did so, he knew it would be terrible and unforgettable because cruelty was the one thing she could not endure; and it begat in her an acid cruelty of tongue that seemed impossible in so gentle a woman.

So he talked. I do not remember what he said but it was simply talk to cover up and appease Aunt Susan's rage, to give Vinnie confidence and to put Henry at ease. He was a man of the greatest intuition and tact and this fact together with his natural kindness was forever putting him into the position of smoothing things over. He achieved his purpose now and in a little while we were all talking naturally and presently old Job Tucker and his wife came over and joined us and in a little while the group around us grew. That some of the joiners came for ignoble reasons was certain, because my grandfather was important and because Job Tucker, his friend, was the richest farmer in the Valley. The exhibition did not make Aunt Susan happy, but presently my grandfather was telling stories of a trip through Africa he had made long ago and the little circle gathered around us grew until it was impossible for those on the outside of the circle to hear him. And as he talked as if quite unconsciously, he put one hand about Vinnie's shoulder. She gave him a single quick glance of understanding, a brilliant glance which illuminated her whole spirit, bringing to me a sudden swift understanding of the great depth of feeling and character which lay beneath the flat face and high cheekbones of the ugly-beautiful face.

I knew then that everything was all right and that my grandfather had miraculously turned whatever ugly thing had happened to advantage and I understood how right he was and in such a situation how wrong would have been Aunt Susan's quick temper and cruel tongue. I knew then it was all right and I slipped away to join the other boys who I knew were somewhere in the caves exploring. I could not bring myself to go until I was certain that everything was all right with Vinnie and Henry.

On my way through the churchyard I saw Old Virgil, withered and sinister, sitting alone at one of the tables. As I passed he said, "You ain't seen Emma Kleinfelter, have you, bub?"

I answered, "No," and as I turned through the gate toward the caves he called after me, "If you

91

see her, tell her I want to go home. Like as not, she's giggling with the girls." He kept on mumbling but I did not hear the rest of what he said.

Through the black shadows and the moonlight and the rocks I made my way back to the main cave. The scent of the foxes grew stronger as I neared the cave and once out of the shadows I started up a doe and fawn which leapt up the hill through the moonlight and black shadows. At the entrance to the cave I pulled out my own candle-end, lighted it, went down on my hands and knees and crawled into the opening. Then, clumsily, I dropped the candle and it went out and at the same time I heard a strange and what at first seemed to me an unearthly noise of moaning. The hair rose suddenly on my head and goose-pimples over the whole of my body. I thought "The story is true! The place is haunted!" And then I heard a man's voice to which the moaning seemed an accompaniment, a voice which was cursing and using the vilest of language in a wild and passionate way. It was a voice which sounded familiar and after a moment I recognized it. It was Red McGovern's voice. But not his voice. It was different as if he were wild with anger, yet even anger did not describe its quality. For a moment I listened and then abruptly both the moaning and cursing ceased and there was only a complete stillness, like the stillness of death, broken only by the sound of a single stupendous sigh.

I wasn't frightened any more in the way one is chilled by the fear of the supernatural, but I was confused and horrified by something I did not understand. I thought, "Perhaps Red is killing someone in there," not knowing that the sounds I had heard indicated something which was a little like death itself. And I thought, "I must run and tell someone." And at the same time I thought that I must not make a fool of myself and that the only person I should tell was my grandfather. I knew that there was something about the whole thing which I did not understand and that somehow there was a likeness in what I had heard to what I had seen on the mornings when the lovesick stallions, trembling and crying out, had bred the mares.

Still confused, I crept out of the cave's opening and made my way in the moonlight and black shadows, as rapidly as possible down the steep hillside through the rocks and trees.

I found that some of the older people were already packing up and leaving. The group around my grandfather had broken up. Aunt Susan was talking with Vinnie and two or three of the more settled and kindly women. My grandfather was still talking to old Job Tucker and to Mr. Peckenbough who lived over the hill. I went quickly to him and tugged the edge of his coat and looking down, he asked, "What is it, son?" And then in the flickering light from the gasoline flares hanging on the trees, he must have seen something in my face and said to his friends, "Excuse me a minute, boys?"

Putting his arm about my shoulder he moved with me into the shadow and asked, "What is it, son? What's happened?"

"I think Red is killing someone." And breathlessly I told him what had happened to me and described what I had heard.

"You're sure it was Red's voice?" he asked.

"Yes. I'm sure. I'm really sure."

He was silent for a moment and then he said, "Red wasn't killing anyone. I think I know what it was." Again he put his arm around my shoulder and said, "Forget it, son. Just come along with me and act as if nothing had happened."

Together we moved across the churchyard in the shadow away from the crowd, until we were on the side next to the hill and the caves. There, he seated himself on a rock where he was hidden in the shadow of a thick shrub and drew me down beside him, holding me closely against his chest.

He said, "If I know Red, we won't have to wait long." And then, "But boy, your heart's beating like a triphammer. There's nothing to be afraid of. Just believe what I say is true. I can't go into

94

it all right here. I'll explain it all to you tomorrow or tonight maybe when we get home."

Then he was silent, listening, and the intensity of his listening imposed itself upon me so that I too remained utterly still, scarcely breathing. And then suddenly we heard the giggling of a woman. It was an hysterical kind of giggling, and then quite close to us the sound of a man's voice—Red's voice unmistakably this time—saying, "Stop that goddam giggling! If you don't stop it I'll never do it for you again." The sound of giggling continued and then the sound of footfalls on the dry leaves and sticks quite near and Red's voice again, "D'you hear me? Shut up! D'you want people to know what's happened? The old man would whale the hell out of you if he guessed."

Then they passed us and their figures were silhouetted against the light of the gasoline flares and I recognized both figures. The man with his short, compact, muscular body and bowed legs was Red all right and the girl, taller with a thick, plump, clumsy body was Emma Kleinfelter, Old Virgil's hired girl.

They separated suddenly and the girl went straight ahead disappearing into the shadow of the church and Red took a different course, edging his way in the shadows to the opposite side of the churchyard where he became lost among the horses

95

and the rigs which were beginning to move away as the party broke up.

My grandfather said, "It's what I was afraid of." He stood up and said, "Come! It's time to go home. Don't ever tell anyone what happened tonight, not even your Aunt Susan. We'll talk it over when we get home."

When finally we started home there were, of course, two rigs—the surrey which Aunt Susan had driven over to fetch Henry and Vinnie and the dogcart which my grandfather and I had used. My grandfather said, "You go with your Aunt Susan so she'll have company on the way home." This suited me because I could ride part of the way home with Henry whom I hadn't seen very often lately, but my joy was complete when Henry said, "Come on, Ronnie. Ride in front with me. We'll let the ladies have the back seat where they can gab."

So I climbed happily in beside him and we drove off out of the black shadows of the great Norway spruce on to the long, dusty ribbon of the Valley road.

The great red harvest moon was high in the sky and the dust raised by the rigs ahead of us hung like a ribbon in the still moonlit air. The horses turned skittish in the first breath of frostiness which had come with the full moon. The rich, fertile smell of pollen from the cornfields was gone now and from the wide, rich fields there arose a different fragrance, less heady, of the ripening corn. Where the road crossed the bridge over the creek the water, spilling over the low dam, was like molten silver.

Henry and I rode silently, Henry giving his attention to the horses while I kept thinking, confused and puzzled, of what had happened in the cave. Behind us Vinnie and Aunt Susan were talking of pickle recipes. Once a little time after we crossed the bridge, I shuddered violently and Henry, noticing me, said, "Chilly?" and quietly slipped his free arm about my shoulder and drew me near to him, holding me tight against his body.

I hadn't shuddered from the cold or from what had happened in the cave. It had happened more and more often lately and, very dimly, I was aware that the shuddering had something to do with my growing up and the changes which were going on inside me. But I was blissfully happy with Henry's arm about my shoulders and the warm feel of his body against my own. There was in the satisfaction, I think, a great deal of the feeling experienced by a cuddling puppy, and presently I began to feel very sleepy and to dream.

At Henry's farm Vinnie and Henry got down and my Aunt Susan moved into the front seat. Henry asked us in for some coffee but Aunt Susan said it was too late and that I was a young boy and must have some sleep. To Vinnie she said, "Get in the cucumbers tomorrow and put them in a stone jar of salt water to soak and I'll come over on Friday and help you put them up."

It had been a happy evening in the end and Aunt Susan had accomplished the first step in her campaign to make the whole of the Valley accept Vinnie. I didn't realize then how tough a campaign lay ahead of her, although I'm sure Aunt Susan knew, for she knew all those farm women, the good ones, the bad ones, the kind ones, the indifferent ones, and although she had never married and had certainly had no very profound experience with love, she understood, with her bright, clear brain, the various resentments they held against a woman like Vinnie. Merely being a stranger was bad enough, but to be a stranger and a foreigner with dyed hair whom Henry had "found at the Fair" made the situation infinitely more difficult.

There were some of the bad, unhappy and thwarted ones who hated Vinnie for all she had been and all the life she had known—a life which in other circumstances they might themselves have led, perhaps gladly; but these delights and that freedom, the more tempting because they had never known them, tormented them and made them hate Vinnie, and the older they grew and the more

remote the prospect of their ever knowing more
than the crude, functional embraces of their busy
farmer husbands, the worse the torments grew.
And there were those who hastened to choose
Vinnie as a symbol for those women who, they
knew in their hearts, had lured their husbands
and their sons into some dim second-floor room
when the men went to Masonville or St. Louis or
Alton. And there were others who, rightly perhaps, felt that the coming of a woman like Vinnie
to the Valley could only lead to disaster since they
knew, instinctively, that a woman like her did not
belong in the Valley and had no place there. Of
course what none of them knew, or could know,
was that the past of Vinnie, whatever it had been,
was an accident and that Vinnie belonged there
more perhaps than any of them, with a peasant's
love of the soil and of the animals which few of
them as "Americans" ever knew. They were right
perhaps in their resentment or at least the resentment was inevitable and understandable, and I
think Aunt Susan understood it well enough. But
there was one thing which both my grandfather
and Aunt Susan would never tolerate and that was
deliberate cruelty to a human or an animal. That
was a thing which could turn either of them into
symbols of granite-hard retribution in which even
they could become as bitter and as cruel as the

blindness of that justice which claims an eye for an eye.

Of course I did not think of these things as I rode sleepily beside Aunt Susan back up the Valley. I have thought of them as I tell this story, looking backward seeing the two of us, a crisp, virginal, very bright old lady and an adolescent boy driving behind Polly, the chestnut mare, and Hector, the black gelding, along the moonlit road. I think I knew then only that Aunt Susan had won the first move in the game and had already begun the second which had to do with the pickles. I even saw through that one. Aunt Susan was going to see to it that Vinnie's exhibit of pickles and preserved fruits would be the best at the County Fair. If Aunt Susan had chosen to enter exhibits, she could have won hands down any year, for even in making pickles and preserves, brains and character have a great place. But Aunt Susan had long ago decided that these things made her *hors de concours* and did not compete and besides, she had many other activities, like her birds, which she found more interesting.

As we rode I felt no puppy impulse to cuddle against Aunt Susan. One might as well have tried to cuddle against a stiffly starched antimacassar. By the time we had reached the gate of the long avenue with the arch reading "Clarendon Stock Farm" I was asleep. I wakened only at the sound

of the bell, a brass bell on a pole, which Aunt
Susan rang vigorously to waken Jasper to come
and take the horses. He came out sleepily, took the
horses and bade us good night.

My grandfather was still up, sitting in his library
with the Bourbon and soda he had each night as
a nightcap. As he heard the door close, he called
out to us and when he stepped to the door, he said,
"You did a good job tonight, Susan."

"You, too, Tom," she said, "I don't think it's
going to be as hard as I thought."

He smiled and said, "I wouldn't be too optimis-
tic." Then he said, "You run along to bed, Susan. I
want to speak to Ronnie for a minute."

She bade us good night and then as she turned
away, she said, "Oh, I forgot to tell you. Vinnie
is going to have a baby. I thought you'd like to
know."

"That's wonderful," my grandfather said. "It's
the best thing that could happen."

Then Aunt Susan rustled away in her starched
petticoats and after looking at me for a second,
my grandfather said, "Come over here," and took
me between his knees and said, "You're getting to
be a big fellow. I hadn't noticed before. Are you
sleepy?"

I told him that I wasn't, that now I was wide
awake.

"I thought I'd better have a word with you so

you wouldn't be lying awake trying to puzzle things out."

He took me by both arms and looked at me directly, so directly that, with all the confusion in my adolescent heart, I felt suddenly abashed and looked away from him. Then he said, "You mustn't let what happened tonight disturb you. What you stumbled on was a perfectly natural thing. It was too bad that it had to be two people as brutal as Red and that girl. You mustn't think of it like that. It can be that way . . . you know from living about the farm and the stables. You mustn't be afraid or ashamed and confused."

He paused for a moment I think because he was finding it so difficult to bring to a small, inexperienced boy the wisdom and knowledge of a long lifetime of experience. "Do you understand what I'm trying to say?"

"Yes, Grandad, I think I do."

My heart was fuller of gratitude for him at that moment than it had ever been. Sometimes I have thought that I was more fortunate in having him for a foster parent than I would have been with my own long-dead father who might have been shy and awkward as fathers often are with sons. In many ways my grandfather and I were closer than fathers and sons ever are. He was so old and so wise that he treated me, intellectually at least, as an equal. He could talk to me simply of things which for him were long since dead and no longer touched him. This a father only a generation older could not have done.

"I didn't want you to worry over it. What you stumbled on tonight," he said, "was ugly . . . ugly and sad. But it can be much better than that . . . much, much better. That is something you will discover when you're older. You must always remember that. The poor girl, you see, isn't very bright. She can't help being that way and she can't help what happened to her tonight any more than the mares can help it. It is Red who is wicked. That too you'll understand some day." He sighed. "But even he can't really help himself. You see, Ronnie, we're all pretty helpless."

He squeezed my arms and said, "Now go along to bed and get a good night's rest. And if there's anything else that puzzles you, just ask me." He laughed, and added, "You see, this is man's talk. That's why I had to send Aunt Susan to bed."

As I left the room, he said again, "And remember, never tell anyone what happened. It might lead to terrible things not for us but for others in the Valley."

I went to bed but in spite of all his kindness and gentleness, I could not sleep. In the darkness, I lay puzzled and a little terrified. I had a curious frightened feeling that this thing of which I had been so unaware until this now waning summer, was closing in all about me. It seemed to be there on every side, wherever I turned. Sleepily I wished that I had Henry there beside me, his warm body close to mine as it had been during the long ride in the surrey. But Henry too was caught now by the same thing which was the same but different. It was not I but Vinnie who lay beside him and Vinnie was going to have a baby. I thought, "Even now . . . at this moment. . . ." And then I fell asleep.

In the morning I had already nearly forgotten what had happened the night before although today the memory of it is as clear as at the moment I heard the moans and cursing in the dark cave. Perhaps that is so because all of us remember forever with unbelievable vividness those things concerned with love and death which happen to us as children before we have had the experience to understand them. All of us have, even as old men or women, brief sharp memories remaining out of the fogs of childhood like beacon lights—the night a brother or sister was born or the first sight of a dead friend lying alone in a shut-up parlor or the picture of two figures in tight passionate embrace in a door or the cry of a stallion in the night. Perhaps it is that the vividness of these memories returns as we grow old and pass beyond that period of torment when we are neither discoverers nor rememberers, but have been instead the mere instruments of something stronger than ourselves. For in one way or another we all are instruments whether driven as directly and brutally as Red McGovern or whether we deny it all and pay the penalty that poor shrivelled Mattie was paying in the stuffy, evil-smelling room in Old Virgil's house.

But on that morning, the sun was shining brightly and the air cool with the first touch of autumn, and so I hurried through my breakfast, feeding part of it to Prince who waited impatiently for me to leave the house for the out-of-doors. There was excitement in the air for Wayne Torrance was coming for two days. I would have driven into Masonville with one of the colored boys to fetch him but my grandfather had not wakened me, because he wished me to sleep late, and so there was nothing to do but kill time until he arrived.

And so, after the quick breakfast, Prince and I ran out to the stables. It was always pleasant there with the smell of fragrant hay and horses and the young foals and the colored boys singing and joking. We went straight to the great mows above the box stalls for I knew it was the hour when Jasper, who cared for the newly foaled mares, would be getting down their hay. He was there, carrying the great forkfuls of fragrant timothy to the chute which descended into the runway below. I took a fork and helped Jasper.

We had worked for perhaps five minutes when the sound of voices below attracted our attention. They were angry voices, one of them my grandfather's and the other that of Red. They came up the chute very clearly so that it was possible to hear every word. Jasper heard them first and at the edge of the chute he stopped with his burden of hay poised in the air, listening. Then he grinned and whispered, "It's your grandpappy givin' Red all hell."

There was nothing for me to do but listen so I too put down my fork of hay and waited, watching Jasper's face which expressed a changing and almost excruciating delight. Red sometimes was arrogant with the colored boys, although never in my grandfather's hearing, and now Jasper was pleased that he was catching it.

My grandfather said, "You ought to be ashamed of yourself." And Red's voice came back, "What I done was natural, Judge. I ain't denying it happened. What's there to be ashamed of? You was a young man once yourself, Judge!"

"That's not what I'm talking about," said my grandfather. "I'm talking about taking advantage of a girl like that who isn't very bright. It's probably never happened to her before."

Red gave a short, vicious laugh, "Mebbe she

ain't very bright but she knows what it's all about. And I wasn't the first one, Judge. She's had plenty of experience. And as to runnin' after her, it wasn't me that did the runnin'. I can't drive past Old Virgil's place without her runnin' out of the house to stop me. She must hang around the window lookin' for me."

There was a silence and my grandfather said, "Well, after this why don't you take another road . . . if you're so scared of her." Then in the midst of his anger, he chuckled, "I must say, it's a funny idea, you being chased . . . instead of doing the chasing."

And Red's sullen voice. "Well, that's the way it is. I ain't lyin'." Then, as a kind of afterthought he said, "And you ought to know, Judge, that living like this, way out here in the country away from everything, you have to take what you can get sometimes. I've never got mixed up with the darkies the way some folks might."

"That's what I've been trying to tell you," said my grandfather. "What you do when you go to St. Louis or Alton or East is none of my affair and I don't care if you want to be a God-damned goat. But keep it out of the Valley. It'll only mean trouble, especially with a girl like that Kleinfelter girl. You wouldn't want to marry her, would you?"

"Hell, no!" said Red.

"Well, it could happen!"

But the threat didn't seem to trouble Red. He only answered, "I'd get out . . . quick!"

There was another pause and then my grandfather said, "Well, Red, we've wasted enough time about this. I just want to say one more thing. You're the best trainer and driver on the Circuit and I don't want to lose you but if this comes up again, you'd better take one of those offers you're always getting."

The threat seemed to subdue Red a little for in a quieter voice, he said, "All right, Judge. I sure don't want to leave. I'll take your advice."

But even then, I knew, as my grandfather surely knew, that Red meant not a word of what he said. He was one of those small, wiry men, almost wholly animal who went his way, untroubled by morality or gossip or even decency. It was one reason, perhaps the principal one, why he understood the stallions so well.

There was no more talk from below and after listening hopefully for another moment or two Jasper divined that my grandfather had gone away, and spitting on his hands, he rubbed them together with a peculiar zest, picked up his heavy forkload of hay and tilted it down the chute. Then he said, "That Red! He just can't keep his pants buttoned! It sure is gonna get him in trouble one of these days." And despite the fact of his dislike for Red, his voice was rich and warm with male admiration.

But the worst had happened for now Jasper knew as much as Red and my grandfather and I knew. He wouldn't even wait out the morning before returning to the cabin to spread the gossip. By nightfall every colored man and woman and a good many of the children would know that Red was in trouble again, this time with the Kleinfelter girl who worked for Virgil Plotz. The only safeguard was that the gossip might never get beyond the quarters of the colored folk, for there was little relationship between them and the farmers of the Valley. The farm was in the border region, neither north nor south, where the status of colored people was a peculiar one, possessing neither the paternal basis of relationship that characterized the country south of us nor the independence that existed in the cities to the north. They were a kind of peculiar phenomenon existing in a "Never-Never-Land" from which they emerged only when some of them went on tour with the horses for the Grand Circuit races.

I helped Jasper put the hay into the box stalls where there were mares and young foals and while we worked I heard from time to time the wild, savage neighing of the two young stallions, Big Pete and Solomon's Choice, in the nearby stall. This sound had a curious quality of urgence and frustration which I knew well. It meant that somewhere nearby there was a mare to be bred.

Then I remembered suddenly that Wayne Torrance would be arriving and was perhaps already at the house and put down my fork, called Prince who was sniffing for mice and set out for the house.

As soon as I entered the house I knew that he had already arrived for in the hall there was a trail of scent that since I had been a very small boy I always identified with him. It was a scent compounded of good cigars, eau-de-cologne and tweeds with something else, the indefinable but disturbing odor which I only understood later, long after his death when I heard a woman in describing a man say, "You can almost smell the sensuality." Very likely it was less an actual scent than some less tangible evidence derived from the instincts, which became associated with the other scents of cigars and cologne water and which carried over in the memory even when he was not present. I know that the peculiar mixture of cologne and cigars, whenever I encountered it in after life, always brought back the memory of Wayne Torrance. It was undoubtedly that curious, intangible, indefinable element, linked with an exuberant health and vitality, which made him attractive to men and sometimes irresistible to women. It explained much of his popularity as a politician and much of his success as a lawyer, for I know now that he was less brilliant, less clever than he had the reputation of being. It was simply that his mere presence in a room seemed to charge the air with excitement, lifting the quality, the interest, the importance of what was said or what happened there to a level many degrees higher.

This quality was very different from that of Red for the sensuality of Red was an aggressive, active, direct force like that of an animal which afflicted most strongly and directly primitive women like the Kleinfelter girl and repulsed the more intelligent and subtle women. With Wayne Torrance, the effect was quite different—the difference perhaps between sensuousness and sensuality. And Wayne, being clever enough and full of intuition, very likely understood the power and used it, deliberately and with calculation. His morality and his conscience were no better than those of Red, but with Wayne the lack of these things was infinitely more dangerous.

But that morning I understood none of this. I only knew that the scent in the big hallway filled me with excitement and hastened my steps along the hallway to the library.

He was sitting there, sprawled out in one of the big leather chairs, for he was as tall as my grandfather, but of a different build, big and muscular, where my grandfather was the lean, hard type who weighed no more in his seventies than he had at eighteen. The feeling of excitement aroused by the trail of scent in the hall was heightened in his presence. At sight of my small figure in the doorway, he sat up and put down his glass of Bourbon, giving me as much attention as if I were the most important man in the world.

"Well, Buckaroo! How are you?"

I went over to him to shake his hand and he took both my shoulders in his big strong hands and held me at arm's length saying, "Growing too! I see you'll be shaving before we know it."

At this remark I blushed furiously. He freed my shoulders and with one hand, rumpled my hair as he said, "I've got something for you. I had to argue your grandfather into letting you have it. I think you're old enough. Bring that parcel over there."

I fetched the long parcel wrapped in cardboard and heavy paper, breathlessly guessing that it might be a twenty-two calibre rifle.

Quickly he ripped the heavy cord off the package. It *was* a rifle, sleek, new and shiny—what I had desired more than anything in the world. I had wanted the rifle not only for itself but as a symbol of freedom. If my grandfather thought I was old enough to carry a rifle safely, then I would be old enough to wander off alone into the swamps at the end of the Valley, a part of the Wild Country.

I looked at my grandfather and saw that he was grinning and in the grin there were many things

—the memory of his own pleasure as a boy over his first rifle, the pleasure he found in my pleasure and the pleasure he found in Wayne, the country boy he had virtually adopted and had educated and who had turned out so well and fitted into our curious little family, almost as if he had taken the place of my drowned father.

He said, "You'd better be careful how you use it. And you'd better never let your Aunt Susan catch you shooting at her birds. She won't mind the crows, of course, but I doubt if you'll ever get a shot at them. They're too smart."

Then Wayne, sensing with his curious intuition that I was burning with impatience to use the rifle, said, "I brought some targets, too. They're in the other package."

I took up the package and found inside a hundred or more paper targets and a dozen boxes of cartridges. Wayne finished off the Bourbon and said, "We might as well try out the gun. Where shall we go, Judge?"

My grandfather said, "The orchard. That's the safest place for a couple of greenhorns like you. The ledge of rocks will stop your wild shots."

Wayne stood up and said to my grandfather, "Will you come along?" But my grandfather said, "No! I've got some work to do. You boys go and enjoy yourselves." And vaguely I felt grateful to him.

I wanted the fun of going out alone with Wayne

and the gun without my grandfather, much as I loved and admired him. I don't know why this was so. Wayne knew it. As I said he had a curious and acute intuition, part animal, I think, which may have been derived from his vitality and his sensuality. He seemed at times not only to divine your thoughts but to anticipate what you were about to say.

We fastened the targets against the trunk of an ancient apple tree and I fired the first five shots. As a greenhorn I handled the gun awkwardly and missed the target paper altogether on three of the shots. On the other two I hit the paper but missed getting inside any of the black rings. Between each shot, Wayne kept explaining to me how to hold the rifle and how to sight it properly.

Then Wayne took the rifle and said, "Now I'll show you how easy it is when you know the tricks."

He raised it in his big, loose-jointed way and fired five shots in quick succession. Three hit the bull's-eye directly and two pierced the paper less than half an inch from dead center, and my admiration for him swelled to new heights.

Then as he finished firing and said "See!" the sound of the stallions' wild and savage neighing came up from the direction of the stables and he said, "Oho! What's up? Shall we go and see?"

I didn't want to leave the rifle and the target but I politely agreed. He said, "We can go on with the shooting later." And with the rifle under his arm and with me following reluctantly he started in the direction of the stables.

I knew what was happening. They were about to breed one of the mares. It was always done at this season if possible, so that the foals would be born in late spring when they would have the advantage of warm weather and the mares of the good summer bluegrass pasture. The operation always took place during the morning, and, at the lane leading to that part of the stables where the breeding took place, there was a painted sign which read: "Ladies not admitted until after 1 P.M."

Wayne walked very rapidly over the rough ground so that it was difficult for me to keep pace with him. As we passed the sign and came in sight of the breeding paddock, Jasper was leading out a chestnut mare with a white blaze and four white feet called Clarendon Maisie. She was a young mare, never bred before and she kept dancing, sidewise, while Jasper kept talking to her and trying to keep out of the way of her hooves. In the sunlight her coat shone like burnished metal.

As Jasper led her to the opposite side of the corral, Red appeared with the big stallion. We reached the fence at about the same time and Wayne stood there leaning on the top rail with one foot on the lowest rail.

My grandfather had never encouraged my watching the breeding of the mares although he had never forbidden it and indeed it was in the late summer so common an operation, what with mares brought long distances from other stables, that the whole affair had little interest for myself or for most of the people about the place. It was only in the last year as I had begun to grow older that the business had any particular interest for me. Left to myself I would certainly not have abandoned the excitement of target shooting in the orchard to watch what was simply a routine performance. But the choice had not been left to me and I was aware that there was indeed another element involved, what it was or whence it came I did not know, except that it was associated with Wayne. It was something I had caught from him and his eagerness to leave the orchard and hurry to the paddock.

At sight of the young mare the big stallion, long experienced in such things, began to rear violently and to scream and neigh. Red had a long lead rein coiled about his arm which was attached to a snaffle bit in the mouth of the big horse. Until he was well into the paddock it seemed that the stallion in his passionate rearing would drag the bandy-legged little trainer off his feet and fling him aside. But Red knew his business and controlled the big horse until in the middle of the paddock, he partially freed the stallion but still clung to the end of the long lead.

The big horse, still neighing wildly ran for the mare as Jasper leapt out of the way. The mare squealed and struck out with her front hooves and then there began between the two what to a greenhorn would have appeared to have been a wild and vicious fight. The stallion approached her from the side, striking at her neck with his teeth and again and again the pretty mare whirled and kicked at him.

Looming high above me against the fence, Wayne watched with excitement, calling out now and then to Jasper or Red, some joking, lewd remark. Then suddenly the mare's behavior changed from one of fierce defiance to one of coquetry. She no longer kicked and squealed but even moved sidewise against the great stallion. Then at a moment which Red knew well from experience, he called out to Jasper and the Negro boy moved next to the mare and took her head close up and held her. The stallion mounted quickly with a fierce and terrible intensity of bitter compulsion. It was quickly over but in the minute or two of action I was aware of something that was like the fierce passion of the voices I had heard in the cave and at the same time I shuddered violently in a curious flash of understanding and shame, and suddenly I was aware that some violent and decisive thing had happened deep within me and that I was older.

Still conscious of some vague sense of shame I glanced at Wayne. His big, handsome face had become very red and he was breathing as if he had been running hard. I noticed that his hands with the beautifully kept nails were shaking. Jasper was leading away the skittish mare and Red, with the slack rein taken up, was holding the rearing stallion, reluctant to quit the mare, close up by his noble head. He still kept neighing wildly and showing the whites of his eyes as he followed the young mare back into the cool shadows of the stable.

Then Wayne gave a deep sigh, turned away from the paddock and said, "Well, what about getting back to our shooting?" But my eagerness was gone now and all at once I was afraid of Wayne. I did not know why. It was as if a cloud had come over the sun.

At lunch, Aunt Susan said, "I'm going over Friday to spend the day with Henry's wife to help her with the canning. Maybe you'd like to drive me over, Wayne . . . you and Ronnie. You might like to meet Henry's new wife."

"Sure," said Wayne, "the Judge wrote me he'd gotten married. He's a good boy. I hope he picked well. He deserves it."

My Aunt Susan spoke quickly, "She's a fine girl. I don't see how he could have done better." It was as if Vinnie were becoming a crusade with her.

We spoke no more about it then and when the coffee was brought in, I said, "How about it, Grandad? Can Prince and I go down to the Wild Country?"

My grandfather hesitated for a moment and then he saw my point—that if I was old enough to have a gun, then I was old enough to go down into the Wild Country.

"I guess it'll be all right."

Then Wayne spoke up. "I'll go along with him. I haven't been down there for years. It'll give me some exercise."

Oddly enough I was disappointed by the proposal. A few hours earlier the prospect of going exploring with Wayne would have excited me, but suddenly I wanted to go alone with Prince and my new rifle.

The Wild Country began below the road which ran along the border of Henry's farm, so in planning out the expedition we decided to drive as far as Henry's place and leave the horses there. Wayne put on an old shirt, a pair of denim pants and some heavy shoes. He borrowed one of my grandfather's rifles, although there wasn't much we could legally shoot at this season—a snapping turtle or a crow or perhaps a snake. Jasper brought around the dog-

119

cart and we put Prince up between us and set out. As we drove along the road down the Valley, my excitement grew. I felt like Cortez or Vasco da Gama, for the Wild Country was a place of mystery many square miles in extent, with great areas of thick overgrown marshland and here and there ridges of primeval limestone rock, honeycombed with caves. Deer roamed the territory and foxes and now and then on the edges of the Wild Country a coyote was killed. It was not so long before that the last bear had been shot.

As Wayne drove, he smoked a big cigar and talked about his own adventures and his boyhood in the Valley on the other side of the Wild Country.

"Your grandad certainly changed my life for me," he said. "Maybe if he hadn't noticed me when I was a kid, I'd still be a backwoods hick. Your grandad is a wonderful man. I'd never do anything to disappoint him."

When we passed Old Virgil's farm the old man and the Kleinfelter girl were out by the barn chasing some strayed hogs. The girl giggled and waved to us but Old Virgil only scowled and looked away as if he hadn't seen us.

"An old skunk!" said Wayne.

But I was thinking of what had happened the night before. The girl was different now. The whole Valley, the trees, the fields seemed somehow different.

As we drove up past the springhouse Henry came out of the house and at sight of us called out a welcome and then, recognizing Wayne, hurried up to the sulky and shook his hand. They were old friends.

I tied Old Ben to the hitching rail and began to unfasten his harness to put him in the cool stable where he'd have hay and be comfortable while we were gone in the big swamp.

Wayne said, "Well, Henry, I hear you've been married. Congratulations!" Then he gave his hearty laugh and said, "Successful?"

Henry's tanned face turned a shade darker. "Yes," he said, "she's a wonderful girl."

"So I've been missing something, huh?" said Wayne.

"If you ask me, yes."

"Well, I guess I'm not the marrying kind. Can't seem to keep my mind long enough on one girl. Have a cigar?"

Henry took the cigar, put it into the pocket of his clean gingham shirt, and said, "I'll keep it till after supper."

"When am I going to see the girl?" asked Wayne, with a kind of impatience in his voice.

"She ain't here now," said Henry. "She's gone to Masonville to buy some things. She and Miss

Susan are canning tomorrow all day. I guess Miss Susan is teaching her some tricks. She's a good cook but she hasn't got the knack of canning, at least not the new-fangled way. You see, her folks are Polish."

Wayne laughed, "I had a Polish girl once. In some ways the finest girl I ever had. They're a very, very loving people . . . very loving. Any additions to the family?"

Again Henry's face darkened. "No. There ain't really been time but we're expecting something next winter or early spring."

Wayne slapped him heartily on the back, "Good boy! Haven't lost any time."

By now I had Old Ben free of the shafts and a halter on his head and I understood something I'd never understood before—the difference between the two men whom I had admired most of any men I knew in the world. Most of all I knew suddenly why everything had changed between me and Wayne since that very morning. One of them was clean like the crystal water from the spring just below the hill. The other was corrupt, although I doubt that at that age I would have known what the word really meant.

Then Wayne said, "Why don't you join us, Henry? You've got nothing to do this time of year." And my heart leapt. I didn't want to go alone with Wayne into the swamp. But almost at once my delight faded away for Henry said, "I'd like nothing better but I've promised to help a neighbor with his wheat. I'm tradin' help."

"Well, if we get lost and don't come back you'll know where we are and send out a search party. It's a long time since I've been in the Wild Country. I doubt if I know my way around."

Henry laughed, "I guess you won't have any trouble."

I put Old Ben in the barn and pitched in some of Henry's good hay and when I came back Henry was bringing out his big team of Percherons. He jumped from the ground on to the back of one of them, smacked it over the rump and said, "Giddap." Over his shoulder he said, "Sorry to leave you boys but Cy'll be waitin' for me. I'm late already."

We stood for a moment watching him and the big team as they moved off down the long lane leading to the woods.

"A fine fellow," said Wayne. "I'm glad he's got himself a good wife."

Then we set off down the slope, crossed the road and went into the swamp where the creek flowed beneath the bridge. Unless you found a deer trail, the creek was the easiest way to get into the Wild Country for you could follow the creek bed, moving from one bank of sand and gravel to another, sometimes wading in the water up to your knees. The water didn't matter for it was a warm day and we were dressed for it.

Once we were into the swamp I wished we had brought fishing rods instead of guns for the stream was full of bass, sunfish and big minnows which skittered away in bright shoals as we moved from one pool to another. Wayne went ahead. He did not move easily with the agile, compact strength of Henry's smaller body. Instead of slipping through the willows and the reeds as a wild creature or a real woodsman would have done, he forced his way through by brute strength.

It wasn't the way I had planned my first expedition into the Wild Country. I knew that crashing headlong through the swamp was not the way to see things. At least it was not my way nor Henry's. I kept thinking how different it would have been if I had come with Henry instead of Wayne. With Henry we could have gone slowly and quietly, even exercising stealth not in order to surprise and kill but to see and understand. When I went with Henry each hummock, each pool in the clear stream, each sand bar became a thing of interest and even fascination in which there existed some small pattern of the universe. It was Henry who had taught me how to see and to fathom and understand the incredible and infinite variety of the natural world. Moreover he had taught me how to *love* the things I saw and discovered as well as to see and understand them. The swallows nests dug deep into the banks, the foxholes, the crayfish moving in his own watery world, the nests of the bass or the killdeer, so alike, one beneath the clear cool water the other on some high, dry gravel bank, had all come through Henry to be a part of my existence, even of my innermost being so that if all else in life failed me, I should still possess a world of infinite beauty and fathomless variety. That hot afternoon I missed Henry with a sense of loss which was like an ache in the heart.

And here I was plunging ahead breathlessly following Wayne who saw and noticed nothing on the way. In my small boy's way I wondered what pleasure he was finding in the expedition beyond the mere goal of going as far as possible as quickly as possible, crushing everything in his path. Although I was too young and inexperienced then to understand it, I was seeing Wayne in his very essence, and with him countless others who throughout their lives aimed merely at going as far as possible with the greatest possible speed only to drop at the end having been nowhere at all.

Once Wayne halted and made a movement indicating stillness and silence. Then slowly he raised his rifle and fired and I saw the slim, scaly body of a big blacksnake wiggle for a moment and slip into the water without a head. Henry would not have shot the snake which was harmless. Any good farmer knew that a blacksnake was a good snake and the farmer's friend. And once he shot at a big fox squirrel, despite the fact that it was not the season for shooting squirrel. Fortunately he missed.

We had gone perhaps a mile or two when he stopped suddenly and looking up pointed to a ridge of limestone rock which rose out of the thick swamp a little way off. Although the ridge was not high, it appeared from the bed of the creek to be a mountain.

He said, "What about climbing up there? We'd get a view of the whole swamp."

In my disappointment over the failure of the afternoon I agreed heartily and a little further along we found a deer trail coming down to the water's edge by a big, clear pool which seemed to lead toward the ridge. The deer had made the track and the fresh droppings showed that they had been using it lately. So we climbed up the bank and followed it through a thick growth of ferns and wild berries. The trail made the going much easier; without it we could never have made our way through the swampy thicket.

The trail led directly to the ridge, turning aside from it and leading deeper into the swamp. We left it and started climbing the ridge itself, a difficult task because the rock rose abruptly and here and there where it had broken down in pockets, brambles and berries grew in abundance. It took us better than ten minutes before we reached the spot near the top where the rock levelled into a wide shelf overgrown with a carpet of wild flowers. The ridge extended perhaps another thirty or forty feet above the shelf.

As we climbed up to the shelf the whole of the Wild Country lay spread out before us, the swamps, the lakes and the distant hills, blue now in a haze of late afternoon heat. And now at last the afternoon was a success. I stood there like Balboa seeing for the first time the endless expanse of the Pacific. And I marked the place then as my own. I'd come back there again and again. I might even lead Henry to it. But always, it would be my own where I could come alone with no one but Prince.

Panting from our exertions, we lay down on the carpet of wild flowers and Prince flung himself down beside me, and for a long time we lay in silence looking up at the blue sky and the white high clouds scudding across it. Then suddenly Wayne extended one hand and rumpled my hair and asked, "Enjoying it, kid?" and I sat up. I was surprised at what he said for I could not believe that he was feeling what I was feeling, high up above the whole of the Wild Country. Perhaps I did not understand that his enjoyment was one wholly of the senses, born of the warm sun and the soft haze and the scent of the crushed herbs on which we lay. Now that the drive had gone out of him for a moment he had relaxed quickly into pure sensuousness.

We sat for a time in silence and slowly a curious uneasiness began to steal over me. I did not understand what it was or why I experienced it. The feeling had nothing to do with anything. It was simply there—a strange emotion compounded of shyness and awkwardness and *fear*. I wanted to be gone off the ridge, out of the marshes and the Wild Country, back to the open, safe country road. Yet it was not a fear of the place itself. I had never been afraid when I was alone. Each time that Wayne turned to look at me the emotion increased in intensity.

Then abruptly Wayne stood up, sighed deeply, and said, "Well I suppose we'd better go back or Aunt Susan'll be having our heads for being late for supper." I too got up and Prince, at the prospect of moving, began to bark wildly and leap against me. Then Wayne said, "Well, I'll be damned!"

I turned toward him and saw that he was looking at the ground. "I'll be damned!" he said again and leaning over, picked up an object which was perhaps the most unlikely thing in the world to find at this spot. It was a woman's handkerchief, small, square with little pieces of cheap lace inserted in each of the four corners.

Then suddenly he held it up and sniffed it and said, "Nope! No perfume!"

We were both thinking the same thing—wondering how a woman could have found her way through the swamp and up the steep broken sides of the ridge and why a woman should come to such a remote and hidden place.

Then Wayne sniffed the handkerchief again, thrust it into his pocket and said, "Well, here goes!" and slipping over the side of the ledge began the journey downward.

The descent was perhaps even more difficult and dangerous because you kept slipping and sliding. Before we reached the bottom both of us were well scratched and bruised by briars and the sharp edges of the rocks. Following the deer trail we came again to the deep, clear pool and he stopped and said, "What about a swim?" When I hesitated, still driven by the desire to leave the thicket quickly and return to the open country, he laughed and said, "It'll save you the trouble of a bath tonight."

He gave me no choice and began stripping off his clothes. I followed his example and we swam and splashed for a time and then Wayne went into the shallow riffle and lay for a time with his big fair body half submerged in the swift running water with his eyes closed. I watched him for a little time and then, unaccountably, began to shiver violently and climbed up the bank into the horse-tail that grew there in luxuriance and began to put on my clothes. The shivering puzzled me for I was not ill.

As I dressed I kept watching him. For the moment lying there on the sandy riffle with the water rushing over him he seemed to have gone away in spirit and not to be there at all. And as I watched, the feeling of uneasiness increased into one of actual dread. If the difference in our ages had been less, I would have called out "Come on! Let's get out of here!" But I was only a kid. I could not give orders to a man so much older and more experienced than myself.

Then as I tucked my shirt into my trousers I became aware that he no longer had his eyes closed but was watching me. When he saw that I was aware of his regard, he stood up, shook himself rather in the fashion of a big dog, climbed the steep bank and began to dress. As he put on his shirt, he said, "Let's try the deer trail. It may be an easier way out."

So we climbed the opposite bank and followed the trail and soon found that it led in the right direction. In a little while we saw light ahead and presently came out on the high road. It was a trail the deer used to and from the fields where sometimes they pastured with Henry's cattle or raided his grain fields. At the sight of the open country, the sense of uneasiness quickly left me, and suddenly I was happy again, principally because I had found a way into the Wild Country and could now come back again and again, alone or with Henry or Prince but mostly, I think, because I had discovered the ledge high on the ridge where I could go alone and lie in the sun and dream. I resolved never again to return there with Wayne who somehow had spoiled everything.

The sun was already low when we reached Henry's house. He was in the barn milking and Vinnie had not yet returned from town.

He said, "Maybe she's met some womenfolk and is having a good gossip. It's hard for a stranger in the Valley to get acquainted." And there was a certain pride in his voice and his manner that she was beginning to be accepted.

We harnessed Old Ben and drove back along the Valley. The evening was lovely and soft and as we passed Old Virgil's house the Kleinfelter girl came out and waved to us, grinning the familiar half-witted grin. It occurred to me, with a sudden new wonder, that she had seen the sulky coming from a long way off and had come out thinking that the driver was Red.

Grandfather had mint juleps waiting when we

arrived and Aunt Susan had begun the fluttering nervous movements which indicated that we were late and the men must hurry over their drinks. She liked good food and disliked having it spoiled and on such occasions she became more and more bird-like—like a chickadee hopping from limb to limb flirting its tail.

At supper my grandfather asked me about our expedition. I told him all there was to tell, all save the feeling of frustration and fear. Perhaps if I had gone to him afterward and told him about that too, he could have explained many things which would have helped to bring peace to me, but, alas, boys do not do such things. It seems that they must find out for themselves.

Then my grandfather said suddenly to Aunt Susan, "I have had a letter from her. He is very much worse. The cure seems to have done him no good." He was, I knew, talking of Melissa and the always mysterious "He."

A silence followed the remark and then Aunt Susan began making arrangements about the trip to Henry's farm to help Vinnie with the canning. It was decided that we should start early, about seven-thirty so that the two women could get in a good full day's work.

Immediately after dinner, I felt very tired with a numbing weariness, and went off to bed with Prince. I did not remain awake for long but before

I fell asleep one resolution had formed in my mind—that I should see as little as possible of Wayne during the rest of his visit. It was very strange that only that very morning I had been waiting his arrival impatiently, and looking forward to following him about like a faithful puppy. Now everything was changed and he had become a stranger or worse, for he had the power of taking all the delight out of my existence. I slept badly that night, crying out now and then in a persistent nightmare in which I seemed to be lost in the Wild Country. The whole of the marsh was on fire and I was being driven back and back to climb finally up the steep sides of the ridge to the ledge we had found. But when I arrived there the carpet of wildflowers was already aflame and there in the midst of the fire lay a scorched handkerchief with cheap lace inserted in each of the four corners.

But for the pleasure of seeing Henry and Vinnie I would not have driven over to their farm with Wayne and Aunt Susan, for I knew that I should have to drive back alone with him.

It was a brilliant morning and when we drove up before the house, Henry came out of the barn to greet us. Aunt Susan got down with the basket of special spices she had brought along and went into the house and Wayne and I prepared to leave when Henry said, "Wait, I'll call Vinnie. I want you to meet her."

He went to the gate in the fence and called, "Vinnie! Vinnie! Come here a minute!" And after a moment her voice, faintly touched with an accent, came back, "I can't come just now, Henry."

"We could go in," said Wayne, in an odd voice.

But Henry said, "No, that would mean tying up the horse." And he called out, "Come on out, Vinnie! Just for a minute. I want you to meet a friend."

Again there was a silence and then Vinnie appeared and walked down the brick path toward us. I was aware of something odd in her walk, almost as if she were lame. She seemed to drag one foot after the other. She came through the gate without looking at Henry and I thought she was angry at him for calling her from her work. Wayne got down from the surrey and met her half way and then I saw that her face was unmistakably white, even under the tan she had acquired from working in the fields with Henry.

Henry said, "This is my friend, Wayne Torrance." And to Wayne he said, "This is my wife!" He was very proud of her.

They shook hands and Vinnie said, "Pleased to meet you." And Wayne said, "It's sure a pleasure to meet Henry's wife. Henry is an old friend of mine. He's sure done well by himself."

There was a sudden silence while Henry stood

by smiling. And then Vinnie said, "If you'll excuse me, I'll get back to my work."

And Henry said, "You don't have to hurry, Vinnie. You've got all day." But she was insistent. She said, "I've got some pickles on and if they boil too long they'll be spoiled."

Wayne said, "Sure, I understand. We'll talk again when we have more time."

"Good-bye," said Vinnie. And then, in a dead voice "Come again!"

She turned and went quickly into the house. But Henry was disappointed. He said to Wayne, "She's not quite herself. You know how it is when women are having babies. She hasn't been feeling so good and I think that's what it is."

"Sure, I understand," said Wayne. He climbed quickly into the surrey and said, "We'll be back to collect Aunt Susan about six o'clock."

"Better make it after supper," said Henry. "They'll probably be busy up to the last minute."

"All right," said Wayne.

He seemed to be in a hurry to be off, drew up the reins and spoke to Old Ben. As we drove off I saw Henry, returning to the barn, walking slowly in his disappointment. He was one of those people who wanted everybody to be happy and his friends to get on with each other. When anything went wrong, his spirits seemed to collapse and he grew worried and something, which he could not fathom, had gone wrong.

All the way home Wayne hardly spoke at all. He seemed not even to notice my presence beside him. As we passed Old Virgil's place, the Kleinfelter girl was again on the weedy lawn under the big maple tree. She was rocking back and forth in the battered, unpainted old roller-swing and as we passed she grinned and waved and with a sudden gesture, pulled her cotton dress well up over her head.

As it turned out, Wayne couldn't drive back for Aunt Susan in the evening. He said he had some work to get out of the way and took a box filled with papers into my grandfather's office.

"I can get the work out of the way," he said, "and then by the time you're back with Aunt Susan I'll be free to talk."

So I drove over with my grandfather and as we passed Old Virgil's place, he came out and hailed us. My grandfather pulled up Old Ben and Virgil came and stood with one foot on the dashboard.

"Sorry to bother you, Judge," he said, "but I had to speak to you."

"That's all right, Virgil," my grandfather said. "What's it about?"

"It's about that man of yours—the one called Red," he said. As I listened, I was troubled as usual because with Old Virgil's squint, I could not tell whether he was looking at my grandfather or not. "He's been foolin' round Emma Klein-felter. You'd better speak to him. The girl ain't even of age and the county's put her in my charge. I've got to protect her. I can't have her carryin' on."

"It's all right, Virgil. I've already spoken to him. I've given him a good dressing down."

"I just want you to warn him," said Virgil. "You tell him if he comes monkeying around here, I've got a shotgun waitin'. I have enough trouble with that girl already."

I chanced to look at my grandfather and saw that he was angry. I knew all the signs. His bright blue eyes took on a hard glint and the tiny veins over his cheekbones seemed to grow larger and larger. When he was angry he did not shout. He was the kind whose anger shows in the chill quality of his voice.

He said, "Well, Virgil, I'll speak to him again but I don't think you'll have any more trouble."

Old Virgil said, "Well, you tell him that if I killed him there ain't a jury in Missouri would convict me. That'll scare him!"

I thought the interview was finished but my grandfather didn't speak to the horse. He sat silently for a few seconds as if thinking. Then he said, "Are you sure Virgil, that you're protecting that poor dim-witted girl as well as you can?"

The question seemed to startle Virgil. This time he looked away for a second and a dull color came over the weathered, wrinkled skin. Then he said, "I sure am, Judge. I treat her like she was my own daughter."

"That's all I wanted to know," said my grandfather. "Giddap, Ben."

It was nearly dark when we arrived to fetch Aunt Susan. She was waiting for us on the front porch sitting alone in a rocker, her basket neatly packed beside her. But at the sound of our arrival Henry came out through the screen door, picked up the basket and carried it for her down to the surrey. I thought it odd that Vinnie wasn't there.

Henry said, "Vinnie told me to say Hello. She wasn't feeling very well and has gone to bed."

"I put her to bed," Aunt Susan said briefly. Then turning to Henry she said, "I'll be over day after tomorrow. If she goes on feeling like this, I'll take her up to see a doctor in St. Louis. We can't have anything go wrong, Henry, either with Vinnie or the baby." Her voice sounded very tired, a rare thing in Aunt Susan.

The next afternoon Wayne left as he had planned to do. I had managed to keep out of his way most of the day but I came up to the house to bid him a polite good-bye.

Again he rumpled my hair and said, "Well,

Ronnie. We had a good time, didn't we? Especially the trip into the swamp."

"Yes," I said, "and thanks for the gun." It was odd how pleased I was at his departure and then it struck me suddenly that he was always touching me and that he seemed to take pleasure in touching anything. He would caress the smooth skin of an apple or stroke the sleek coat of a mare or even touch and finger the material of a dress that Aunt Susan wore. It was as if the sense of touch was enormously developed in him, as if it more than any other of his senses were his real contact with the outer world.

Jasper arrived presently with the dogcart and Wayne drove away. My grandfather looked after him, smiling and Aunt Susan went into the house.

The summer was nearly over and there were about ten days more to go before I had to return to school. Henry and Vinnie asked me over to spend two days and two nights. Two days after the canning, Vinnie recovered with mysterious swiftness and was in fine health once more. When I saw her again I thought she seemed almost beautiful. Having a baby did not seem to trouble her at all, perhaps because she had the strength of peasant blood. It was Henry who kept her from carrying heavy buckets of milk and from climbing the ladder in the orchard to help him with apple picking.

I remember her sitting on the grass in the brilliant sunlight of autumn, sewing while Henry and I picked apples. She had brought her accordion along and now and then when she grew tired of sewing, she would play and sing for us. The sunlight, striking down from behind her, turned the loose ends of her golden brown hair into a kind of halo about her head and I couldn't help thinking how different she was from many of the native daughters of the Valley, even the younger ones who seemed to hate their lives, to hate the trees and the fields and the very farm animals. Most of them were always talking about when they could get away to the city. Vinnie was clearly so happy among all these things.

And she must have been very happy in Henry's love. I would discover him suddenly watching her as she sat on the grass surrounded by the piles of rosy apples. He would stand there, an apple in his hand, the picking forgotten, watching her, a smile on his face. And then shyly he would come out of the dream and go back to his work.

Both evenings I spent there were cool with a high misty moon and we wore sweaters as we sat on the porch listening to Vinnie play the accordion and singing her "sad sonks." I was blissfully happy for my jealousy of Vinnie was gone now. Somehow in her wisdom she had accomplished this without my losing any of my adoration for

Henry. Like my grandfather and like Henry she treated me always as if I were grown up and somehow she made the friendship and sympathy between Henry and myself expand to include herself, so that presently I began to understand why he loved her so much and even to see little things about her and perhaps about all women which were beautiful—things which as a boy at the age when he despised girls I had never noticed before.

I noticed the beauty of the full bosom under the calico dress and the curious way her lips curved up at the corners and the way her hair turned golden in the light where it grew along the arch of her neck as she bent her head over her sewing and the whiteness of her skin when she moved and the dress revealed suddenly a part of her bosom which was not tanned by the sun.

When I told them about the ledge of rock I had found in the swamps the day I went with Wayne, Henry said, "Sure, I know the place. Remember, Vinnie, I took you there when you first came here?" He turned to me. "I wanted her to see what beautiful country it was. I was afraid she wouldn't like it. Remember, Vinnie?"

"Yes," she said, quietly. "It was very pretty."

"It's the kind of place nobody ever goes to," said Henry. "You couldn't find it unless you stumbled on it. I don't suppose anybody ever goes there."

That made me think of the handkerchief and I told them about finding it and how Wayne had carried it away with him.

"Funny," said Henry. "Funny thing to find in a place like that."

Vinnie didn't say anything at all but suddenly the accordion began to moan softly and she began to sing very quietly in a low voice, and we didn't talk about the place any more.

That night after I had gone to bed there was a knock on the door and I said, "Come in" thinking it was Henry. But when the door opened, it was Vinnie who came in carrying a glass of milk and a plate of cookies.

She said, "I thought you might be hongry."

She put down the milk and cookies on the table beside my bed and stood there looking down at me. "We're going to miss you, Ronnie. Too bad you have to go so far away to school."

"I'll miss you, too, Vinnie," I said. "Thanks for the stuff."

She said, "I understand, Ronnie. I didn't want you to think I didn't. I know you hated me when I first came here and I know why. It ain't made any difference, *has* it?"

"No, Vinnie. It's different, but it's nicer."

"Good . . . I'm glad. I wanted to be sure."

Then, without a word, she bent down and kissed my cheek. I could not remember my mother and my Aunt Susan was not the type given to showing her affections; when she kissed me it was like the brush of a wren's wing against my cheek. This was the first time a woman had ever really kissed me. It was unbelievably different from Aunt Susan's brisk, little peck. The kiss was filled with warmth and affection and I think pity, and as she bent over me her bosom brushed my chest. A warmth swept through the whole of my young body and suddenly I felt an overwhelming desire to cry and only kept back the tears with the greatest effort. I could feel the color rushing into my face and was glad that there was no light in the room but that of the moon.

"You don't mind, Ronnie?"

"No. It was. . . ." I tried to find words. "It was nice of you."

"Look, Ronnie. If ever you feel lonely . . . you know . . . if you don't understand something and you want to know, ask me about it. I think now we understand each other." Then she touched my hair, very lightly and said, "Good night, now. Don't try to read tonight. Maybe you read too much. Too much reading can get people all mixed up."

"Good night . . . Vinnie."

She went out and when she had closed the door I turned quickly and lay on my side, my head buried in my arm to shut out the light of the moon. But I was crying silently and in a little while my arm was wet with the tears which came without any sound . . . I, who never cried because until now I had never had any reason to weep. It was a strange kind of weeping, curiously without shame, in which there was a sense of physical relief as if all the tears I should have shed, all the tears that other children had shed by the time they were as old as I, were coming now all at once. As far back as I could remember I had had security and kindness but I had never had cause to weep and now suddenly I understood that weeping could be a voluptuous and satisfying as well as a painful thing and that we could weep for joy as well as for pain, as well as for those things which were neither joy nor pain but compounded of both and lay somewhere in between.

At last the tears stopped coming and I lay there feeling weary but somehow pure and strong and with a deep sense of the goodness and the richness of life. It seemed very strange to me that Vinnie had known how to do what she had done, how she knew that I had desired this thing for so long without ever knowing it until now. The uneasiness, the sense of a cloud crossing the sun which had plagued me ever since Wayne's visit was gone. But more than that I was wiser and freer than I had ever been.

I left the next afternoon and did not see them

again, until I went off to school but when I opened my bag on the train I found a parcel of homemade cookies with a piece of common ruled paper on which was written "From Henry and Vinnie. Good trip."

Boarding school never meant very much to me. When I look back on it now I find it difficult to remember very much about it. I have a few friendships which have survived but today I have difficulty in remembering the names of most of my schoolmates, even of those I knew well. I must have learned something because I was bright enough, and because of my strange life at home I was precocious and wise beyond my years. I was good enough at games for the good food at Clarendon Farm, a good inheritance and all the swimming and riding and cross country rambling I did there, gave me a strong, solid, and alert body, but I never excelled at any sport because I lacked the interest and had no great sense of teamwork.

Nearly all the other boys were from cities and from rich and sometimes fashionable families and I got on well enough with them because the simplicity and the dignity of my grandfather and Aunt Susan, who were as much at home with ambassadors and bank presidents as with Henry or Vinnie or the other people of the Valley, had given me a sense of the value of people and things, but I could not always understand the great interest with which the other boys surrounded the whole business of sex which seemed to me, outwardly at least and in the mechanics, simple enough. The dirty stories they told were neither very funny or even very interesting to a boy who had spent all his summers on a farm where breeding was a casual and almost daily affair.

So school passed rather in a blur, neither pleasant nor unpleasant, with occasional week ends or holidays spent visiting rich schoolmates or with my grandfather and Aunt Susan in the big house in Washington. My grandfather wrote me serious letters about what was happening in the world and Aunt Susan wrote long and detailed old-fashioned letters filled with gossip and household details and little stories, like the long and rich letters of people before the days of telegrams or telephones or easy traveling. They were the last vestiges of an age and an epistolary style that was rapidly vanishing.

That year she wrote me a long letter in October telling me all about the County Fair and among other things, she wrote:

Vinnie's canning and pickle-making turned out very well. Perhaps I should have written *our* pickle-making and maybe I cheated for Vinnie's sake but the tricks I knew were a help. Her pickles were crisper and a better color than any of the others. The damson jam was really first class and the peaches looked almost fresh in the jars and tasted that way too. Altogether she won seven prizes. Of course the baked things were her own and we didn't cheat on them. I couldn't have helped her with them because she knows a great deal more about them than I do.

I think it's done a great deal for her because most of the other women thought she was a city girl who didn't know anything about such things. We showed 'em. There was some jealousy among some of the older witches like Mrs. August and Mrs. Downes but they couldn't say it wasn't fair because the judges came from State College and didn't know anybody. The decisions were on merit alone.

But you should have seen Henry. I thought he was going to burst with pride. He knew they'd been pitying him in the Valley and talking behind his back because he'd gone out of the Valley to find a wife and, what was worse, had gone to St. Louis for her. And now it turned out that he'd married the best canner, pickle-maker and cake-baker in the whole county—not to mention the way she helped in the dairy and on the rest of the farm when most young women refused to put their foot outside the door. I think everything is going to be all right from now on. We're planning to stay here until the end of November and come back this year about the first of May, so they won't be left alone very long.

Vinnie's feeling bad turned out to be nothing at all, so I didn't have to take her to St. Louis. I did make her go into Masonville to see Dr. Lee and he said he'd never seen a healthier woman or one more designed by nature to be a mother. I must say it seems to agree with her. She looks downright handsome.

Your grandfather has had a cold but is otherwise all right. As you know I can never persuade him that the autumn evenings turn chill when the sun goes down. He said to tell you to bring anyone you like to Washington for the Thanksgiving and Christmas holidays.

And so the letter rambled on with news about Jasper and his family and all the other colored people who lived in the cabins by the stables and about the birds which seemed to be going south early which indicated an early winter. And she mentioned that Wayne had decided to run again for Congress in the fall. My grandfather, she wrote, thought he was sure to get it.

There was much, much more in the letter. The letter was five pages long written on both sides in Aunt Susan's fine, precise, script and at the last page when she found she still had something more to say but not enough to merit the waste of a whole new page, she followed the old-fashioned economical habit of writing *across* the words she had previously written. This was a maddening relic of the days when one sheet cost a penny less to post than two sheets and sometimes it led to confusion as to what she was writing.

But there was one thing which she did not tell in that letter, the most important thing of all which she kept secret until long afterward. It was unlikely that she would have written it to me but she did not even tell my grandfather.

It was what Vinnie had told her on the day they spent together making preserves.

It was this. Late in the afternoon while Henry was still at the neighbor's helping with the wheat, Vinnie had felt suddenly faint and gone into the bedroom to lie down. Aunt Susan had finished bottling the last of the pickles they were working on and had gone into the bedroom with some of the cherry brandy made long ago by Henry's mother, and when Vinnie had drunk a little of it, she covered her face with her hands and said, "Miss Susan, I have to tell you something."

I am sure that Aunt Susan knew what was coming and the knowledge made it easier for her to help Vinnie tell it. It was astonishing how an old maid like Aunt Susan could know so much about the human race and its weaknesses. She said, "Yes, Vinnie. What is it?"

With her face still covered, Vinnie said, "I don't know if I should tell you."

"You can tell me anything you like." She reached over and touched Vinnie's hands. "It wouldn't make any difference. I understand more than people think."

"I'm afraid!"

"Yes."

"I'm afraid you might not like me if I told you. I'm afraid you wouldn't want to see me again."

"No," said Aunt Susan, "that won't happen,

Vinnie." And I think Vinnie with that deep instinct of hers believed her.

She said, "Before I came here, Miss Susan, I was a bad woman." Then she took her hands from her face and looked out of the window across the Valley. "I didn't want to be. Only I was just a dumb Polack. I didn't know what to do."

"Tell me, Vinnie . . . if you want to."

And then suddenly the story poured out like water spilling through a broken dam. It was the oldest story in the world. To help out her family, Vinnie had gone to St. Louis to work as a hired girl. She found a place in a good boardinghouse where unmarried professional men lived—lawyers and engineers and men working in the factories. It was a good place and she thought herself very lucky to be earning ten dollars a week with a tiny, hot room under the eaves and the privilege of eating whatever was returned from the tables. She worked as a chambermaid and at meal times waited on table.

She wasn't exactly a pretty girl but there was something about her which was attractive to the men, most of them young and all of them unmarried. Three or four of them asked her to go out with them secretly in the evening but she refused them all but one man with whom she fell in love. There was no doubt about it because Vinnie, even then as a young inexperienced girl, knew what love was. At first she refused to see him but he brought her small but sometimes expensive gifts that meant a great deal to a young immigrant girl earning ten dollars a week and sending nine of it home to her parents and nine brothers and sisters. Finally one night, when she felt tired and discouraged, she agreed to meet him outside.

He took her to a vaudeville theatre and gave her supper afterward. It was his kindness which won her, his kindness and his good looks and a certain warmth and intensity. And he was important too which made her feel childish and ignorant and even flattered that he should notice her. That, of course, was only the beginning. After that she met him two or three times a week and when she had completely lost her head, she went with him one night to a hotel. And after that they went again, and again.

As she told the story to Aunt Susan, she said, "I didn't know what I was doing. I didn't care about anything. I was crazy."

And then she found that she was having a baby and when she told him, he said that he could not marry her because he was an important man. He would see that everything was taken care of and he did send her to a hospital and paid for everything. The baby was born dead and when she was able to leave the hospital, he left some money with her and disappeared. She went back to the boardinghouse but the woman who ran it had found out all about what had happened and would not take her back.

She couldn't find another job and then one night she met one of the other men from the boarding-house and went to a hotel with him. And from then on it went that way. She made much more money than she had made working at the board-inghouse. She wrote to her family that she had a new job and sent them more money. But all the time she hated the life. In the spring the World's Fair opened and St. Louis was filled with visitors and she could have made even more money, but something happened to her. There came a night when she could no longer go on and she decided to go down to the river and drown herself. She was sitting on a bench in the new railway station trying to get up her courage, weeping quietly and trying not to attract attention when a young fellow sat down near her on the same bench. It was Henry.

To Aunt Susan, she said, "He had such a nice face. And he looked so young and he didn't look like a city man. I thought, 'If all this hadn't hap-pened to me. If I'd stayed home, I might have married someone like that.' "

She turned away from him so that he should not see that she had been crying, but he saw it anyway and asked, "What's the matter? Is there something I can do to help you?"

She wanted to go away but something held her back. At first she wouldn't talk at all but presently she told him simply that she was alone in the city and had no job. It was hard talking about such things there in the new, crowded station with people coming and going all about them and people on the bench opposite watching and straining to hear what they were saying. Once a middle-aged man sitting across from them laughed.

Vinnie told Aunt Susan, "I knew what he was laughing at. He thought it was the old story of the whore catching the country boy."

And all the time she talked to him, she was thinking, "If I stop talking to him, if I go away, I'll go down to the river. All the time I was really wanting him to stay because it seemed like that was all I had to hang on to . . . that young fellow sitting beside me wanting to help me some way. It seemed as if maybe God had sent him along just in time to keep me from killing myself."

Then Henry proposed that they go and find something to eat and she said "yes" and took him to a restaurant where she knew the food was good but cheap. And the supper was very pleasant and Henry did most of the talking. He told her about his farm and his horses and all about the people in the Valley and in particular about my grandfather and Aunt Susan.

"He was like a little boy," Vinnie said. "And the more he talked the more I was ashamed of

153

myself with all the things I knew and all the things I had done."

But even in the restaurant, people looked at them—the young farmer and the girl with the brassy, dyed hair, showy feather hat which proclaimed her profession. Henry was so innocent that he didn't notice, but Vinnie saw and heard everything and even then she began to hope that he'd never notice them or find out why they were grinning.

After they'd finished eating, they took a long trolley ride and talked some more and presently Vinnie told him a little about her father and mother and her nine brothers and sisters and how her parents came from the Old Country and her father worked in the mines over in Illinois and she couldn't go home but had to stay in the city and work so that she could send them money and they'd have enough to eat and not be evicted from the company-owned house. With strikes and layoffs it had been worse than ever for the past year.

It was only after all this talk that both of them realized suddenly that they didn't know each other's names and Henry said shyly that his name was Henry Benson. She said hers was Vinnie Kowalski, but she wouldn't tell him where she lived because it was a cheap hotel where she could bring men without anyone making a fuss. She wouldn't let him walk home with her.

"For a moment," she said, "I thought he was going to ask me to go home and spend the night, but I discovered that he'd never thought of such a thing. He was so innocent he never suspected what I was."

So they arranged to meet the next day, and most of the night she lay awake worrying about whether she should keep the bargain. She kept thinking, "It's too late now. If I go on I'll hurt him. I can't change what has happened in the past. I can't ever get rid of it." But at the same time she wanted to see him again and she was filled with the feeling that he alone could change everything and keep her from the river. It wasn't as if she had liked her life. It was a horror to her, and with each day the horror increased, pushing her a little nearer to the brink of things.

In the end she kept the appointment, but before she went she dressed herself in the soberest clothes she had and put on a hat which nearly covered the brassy hair so that people wouldn't look at them and whisper and laugh.

All that day and the next, they spent at the Fair, enjoying themselves until late at night when they rode back again on the trolley and Vinnie got off at her corner and walked home without letting him accompany her. For Vinnie it was like heaven. It was what she had never known. And on the

155

third day he asked her to marry him and go back with him to the farm.

He asked it very simply, saying, "I'm all alone there. We get on pretty well. I think you'd like it. It's a good farm and the Valley's very pretty."

When she didn't answer him, he went on about the place—about his fine cattle and his horses and the wide pastures and orchards and the stream that ran through them and all about the Wild Country and the deer and bear.

"It was like hearing about heaven," Vinnie said. "And all the time I wanted to take care of him. I wanted to milk his cows and make his butter and help him in the fields the way women did in the Old Country."

Presently, frightened and ashamed, she heard herself saying, "Yes," hardly believing any of it was true.

Then Vinnie said, "I had to tell somebody. I've never talked to Henry about my life in St. Louis. I would never tell him because I would kill myself to keep him from finding out. But now I can't kill myself because I'm having a baby and I can't run away because it's Henry's baby too. But I'm afraid . . . all the time, I'm afraid!"

Then Aunt Susan told her it was having a baby that made her feel that way and that she didn't give Henry enough credit for character and goodness.

"What he doesn't know, won't hurt him," she said. "And even if he found out anything, I think the past wouldn't matter now."

She tried to make Vinnie understand how simple a man Henry was and how genuinely good. "I've known him since he was born. I know him maybe better than you do. All that is past now and you've only the future to think of. If anything ever happens you come straight to me and the Judge."

And some part of Aunt Susan, born perhaps out of that mysterious thing which we all vaguely inherit, instinct and wisdom, led her to ask a question.

"That first man, Vinnie? Are you still in love with him?"

For a moment Vinnie was silent. Then she said, "No!" and Aunt Susan asked, "Do you feel about Henry as you did about him?"

And again, slowly, after a silence, Vinnie said, "No. For Henry I would kill myself. I would go through fire and be tortured. You see, Miss Susan, what I feel for Henry is pure." She hesitated for a moment as if seeking words from the pitiful number she knew and used. "It's like the trees and the fields. The other thing was terrible. It was bad. It was like I could not save myself. I had to do what he said. I was like a slave. I didn't have no mind of my own. It was like my body have a fever all the time. It was big—that feeling—it was terrible. And all the time I was afraid like a crazy woman." She looked out of the window and then said, "He knew it too. He knew how to make me do what he wanted. He knew how to make it so I couldn't think of anything but him and wanting to get back to him."

"Do you ever think of him?" asked Aunt Susan.

Again Vinnie hesitated and then in the terrible honesty which was part of the girl, she said, "Yes, sometimes it is like he crept up behind me only he isn't there. And I remember things and I push him away from me like out of my head. Whenever it happens I run out of the house and go and find Henry wherever he is and then the other one goes away."

"Have you seen him since, Vinnie? Do you know where he is?"

Again there was an inward struggle and this time perhaps because the whole thing with all the complications was too much for her simple mind, she lied. "No," she said.

She lied because she had seen him that very morning.

Aunt Susan said, "There's nothing to worry about. He's gone and you don't know where he is and gradually he'll just fade out of your mind."

And because she had lied, Vinnie couldn't answer at all. The confusion, all the relief she had found in pouring out the whole story to Aunt

Susan, suddenly came to an end. A wall rose between them. If she had turned suddenly and said, "It's not true. I have seen him. He's Wayne Torrance!" everything would have been different for Aunt Susan and my grandfather would have stepped in and everything would have been changed for Vinnie and what happened would never have happened. But even Vinnie's honesty was no proof against so many human complications. And perhaps, even in her apparently simple soul there lay, hidden away, the cankerous hope that she *would* see him again, that she would know again that terrible folly and ecstasy which was apart from all else in her life.

It would have been tricking you not to have told you that the man was Wayne Torrance. You might have guessed and been right and detected the trick or been scornful in the end because the story had not been told honestly.

Of course no one knew at that time that the man was Wayne—neither Aunt Susan, nor my grandfather, nor Henry, nor myself. And Vinnie had poured out her heart to Aunt Susan and felt relieved and the next day Wayne went away and Vinnie's odd illness, which had troubled both Henry and Aunt Susan, went with him.

PART III

IN MAY MY GRANDFATHER STOPPED OFF ON HIS
way to Boston and spent the night at the school.
Because he was so distinguished a man the headmaster invited him and me with him to sit at the
headmaster's table. After supper I was invited to
the headmaster's parlor with my grandfather and
after an hour my grandfather said good night and
took me with him into the school library.

We sat in a corner by the fire and he said suddenly, "How would you like to go to Europe for
the summer?"

I thought swiftly of the Valley and the happy
life there and asked, "*All* summer, Grandad?"

"No. You'd be home by the middle of August.
You could come straight to Clarendon. That
would give you nearly six weeks there."

Reluctantly, I answered, "That would be all
right, I guess."

He lighted a cigar and said, "It seems Mr.
Pulsifer is taking some of the boys on the Grand
Tour this summer."

"What's that?" I asked and my grandfather smiled, realizing, I think, the great gap in years between us and that the old-fashioned Victorian expression meant nothing to me.

"The Grand Tour," he said, "used to be a part of the experience of every really educated gentleman. It still ought to be, but it's gone out of fashion. Your headmaster fortunately still believes in it as I do. The Grand Tour is a trip which includes parts of England, France, Germany, Italy and Austria. While on it, young men are supposed to learn at first hand about history and architecture and music and anthropology and even economics and a lot of other things. If we had more men in Washington today who had made the Grand Tour, this country and the world would be a good deal better off. That's why I want you to have it. You see the life you've known up to now has been somewhat narrow—either here at school or in the Valley. Both are nice places but both have limitations. They're both *little* worlds, complete in themselves and the great world is quite different. Mr. Pulsifer, I understand, is well qualified as a guide. He's a very cultivated gentleman who I believe will be able to point out to you what is important. A lot of your friends will be on the trip."

As I listened, I was torn by two desires—one the desire for adventure, however discreet, which the trip offered and the other, a nostalgia for the Valley and the Wild Country which was now open to me, but most of all in the second desire was embedded the images of Henry and Vinnie, for now Vinnie was as much a part of my innermost life as Henry had always been. But I trusted my grandfather and his wisdom.

"When do we leave?" I asked.

"As soon as school is out. I think some time early in June."

I said, "All right, Grandad."

"I'm glad you agree," he said. "It is something for which you will be thankful for the rest of your life."

Then he put down his cigar and frowned, and after a moment's silence, he said, "There's one more thing I must tell you and it's not easy to do." He crossed one long, lean leg over the other and said, "You've heard your Aunt Susan and me often speak of someone called Melissa?"

"Yes, Grandad."

"You never asked who she was but I suspect that you have guessed."

"Yes, Grandad. She's my grandmother, isn't she?"

"That's right. And I know you've wondered why she was always such a mystery and didn't live at Clarendon with the rest of us."

"I didn't know."

He frowned again before he spoke. "You see, nearly thirty years ago your grandmother left me.

It's very difficult to explain these things but as you grow older you'll understand them and I think it's not fair any longer not to tell you. Your grandmother fell in love with another man. I don't think she wanted to fall in love or that she meant to. You see, Ronnie, there is always a point in such cases where one can turn back but your grandmother as a young woman was very beautiful and very headstrong. We were living in Europe then and she was a famous beauty. They always said that people stood on chairs to look at her at the races or at any public gathering. She was not the kind to pull up short while she still had things under control. She fell in love and headlong in love. Maybe you'll understand that too when you're older, although most men never really do."

He laughed nervously and said, "To make a long story short. She had to have her way and for a time I let things ride thinking she would get over it all. But she never did. We didn't get a divorce, at first because I thought things would right themselves, and a little later because a divorce and all the scandal would have wrecked my career and all the things I was trying to accomplish. Your grandmother, you must remember, is a nice woman, even, I think at times, a noble woman and certainly a lady. She didn't want what she considered her mistake to wreck my career. She knew she had hurt me but she wasn't willing

163

to wreck the rest of my life. So she just went on living with the man, quietly and discreetly. I must say in justice to her that the whole affair was neither trivial nor cheap. She has stayed with him all these years although he is old now and blind and ill. In judging her, we must give her that credit. Now, after all these years, I believe that she could not have helped herself. It was something which happened and since she could not help herself, she made things as easy as possible for me. She could live as she did in Europe where it would have been impossible in this country. In Europe there is a whole society of people like that. They live in Paris, in Venice, in Rome, in Florence. It is possible that in the particular situation they are more civilized in Europe than we are in this country where most unhappiness is translated immediately into divorce and scandal."

His face had turned quite grey with the effort he had made in telling me the story. It was as if he were dragging it from the very depths of his soul.

"Your mother and father," he said, "saw her nearly every year. They died on the way home from a visit. She has never been back to America in thirty years. Now the point is that you are going to Europe this summer and it would be unfair not to see her. You are, after all, her only grandchild. I've sent her pictures of you and Aunt Susan has written her about you. I am going to write her to say that you are coming. I'll send the itinerary and she can arrange where to meet you. I want you to be very nice to her. You will probably love her as most men have always done. You must understand that in retribution for what she did, she has given up many things—among them the pleasure of knowing her only grandson." He stood up suddenly with his back to the fire as if he had become chilled by the effort of telling me Melissa's story.

"You understand what I'm trying to tell you?" he asked.

"Yes, Grandad."

"There isn't any question you'd like to ask?"

"No!"

"Well, you'd better go along to bed now. We'll have breakfast together before I go to Boston."

Then he put one arm around my shoulder and walked with me to the door.

"Good night, son," he said.

"Good night, Grandad . . . and thanks."

My roommate was already asleep so I undressed in the darkness and after I had gone to bed I could not sleep for a long time. I was wakeful not because I had been shocked or even surprised by what my grandfather had told me, for some inner part of my young mind had long since divined and accepted it, but because I kept pondering what might lay before me in experience and by the fact that all these strange intimations which had concerned me more and more as I grew older had touched the lives of my grandparents as well. I think that for the first time I began to fathom a little the depths of my own adolescent emotions and how they were related to all of the things I was learning so rapidly—things which touched my relation with Vinnie and Henry, Red and the Kleinfelter girl, my own grandparents and my understanding of them. I began even to fathom a little the feeling of uneasiness which had clouded and complicated my whole relationship with Wayne and his curious way of living wholly through his senses.

On the following day I had a short letter from Henry. He wrote, "Vinnie had a nine-pound boy yesterday. Both are doing well. We're going to name him Ronnie. I thought you'd like to know. She sends her best."

For a second I had a confused feeling that somehow the child was a brother or at least that in some way I had had a part in his existence. It was a curious, warm almost sensual feeling that went away very quickly. I was proud that they were naming the child after me. It was as near as I could come toward the realization of the adolescent feeling I had for both of them, for it was no longer

Henry alone for whom I had a boyish admiration and love. It was Vinnie as well.

I think that for the first time I understood dimly my boyish love for Henry—that all along I had wanted to be *like* Henry. Yet it was more than that. I had wanted to *be* Henry, to *be* his body as well as his spirit and to experience what *his* body and *his* spirit experienced. I now saw that my childish liking for Wayne had been quite a different thing which turned, as I began to grow into a man, into distrust and uneasiness and anguish. I had been jealous of Vinnie because she was a part of that experience of Henry's which I could no longer share and so she shut me away from him. But she had somehow known this and changed it all, transferring somehow deftly by instinct alone some of that strong feeling to herself, so that I became identified in my growing, confused mind not with Henry alone but with both of them. So skillfully had she done this that now for an instant this baby seemed in some way mine as well as theirs. I was certain that it was Vinnie who had wanted to call the baby by my name.

Ten of us left with Mr. Pulsifer on the Grand Tour in the beginning of June. We went first to England then over to France, through the Rhineland, back through France into Italy, leaving Austria until the last. It was a pleasant enough tour on which all of us, I think, learned a great deal. Mr. Pulsifer, as a guide, was thorough and made what we saw interesting, but he did more than that for he managed to make us understand how all of us, although American, were to a very great degree the products of the civilization we were studying and how much we owed to it. My grandfather was right in the assumption that it would change and enrich the rest of my life. How much it affected the lives of the other boys I cannot say, but they cannot have been untouched by it. For me there were perhaps special benefits for it took me away from the Valley and its small, complete, intense life at a time when it was better for me not to become too closely involved. The trip was so crowded with external and objective sensations and experiences that there was no time for the daydreaming, the inward probing and the taste for solitude toward which my own nature and the circumstances of my life inclined me to an exaggerated degree.

In late July in Florence, I found a letter with the postmark Bad Gastein on it waiting for me at Cook's office. It was, I divined, the long-awaited letter from my grandmother. She wrote,

MY DEAR RONNIE:

I know you have been waiting to hear from me and I have not written until now as my plans were very uncertain and I did not know where would be the best place for us to meet. I now find that I shall be staying at Bad Gastein until September and according to the itinerary your grandfather sent me you will be at Salzburg about August seventh. Bad Gastein is only a short distance away and I will arrange to spend a day or two at Salzburg while you are there.

Please note that I will be at the Bristol Hotel where I suppose you and the other boys will be staying as it is the best hotel in the town. I think you will like the countryside and all the lakes and mountains. They are very beautiful. And Salzburg will give you some idea of the times of Maria Theresa and Joseph II. Of course, it was also in a way, Mozart's home. But no doubt your instructor, Mr. Pulsifer, will tell you all about that.

Needless to say, I am very impatient to see you. Your grandfather and your Aunt Susan have been very good about sending me photographs and news of you. I feel that I would know you on sight. Let me know if there should be any change in your plans. The above is the address. With best wishes and much affection.

Your grandmother,
Melissa Stillcombe

The address to which I answered was Villa Weber, Bad Gastein. I wrote her that we would be arriving on the date mentioned and would be staying at the Bristol for one day and then going on to Munich.

From Florence we went to Venice and then to Vienna, and I am glad now that we spent five days in Vienna because that lovely city will never again be as it was before 1914. It was like an Operetta with lovely music and gay uniforms and pretty women and good food and I am sure that the population was better off than it has ever been since or will ever be again, and happier too.

But all the time I kept thinking about my grandmother. What would she be like? How would she look and act? Probably more like a European than an American. How strange and difficult it would be to see and talk to her for the first time. The doubts at times grew so strong that I wished I were not going to meet her at all.

We arrived in Salzburg about eleven in the morning and when I asked the porter whether there was a message for me he gave me a note addressed in my grandmother's handwriting. It read,

MY DEAR RONNIE:

I am sorry not to have been here to greet you but I had some urgent errands to do. I have taken a table for lunch at the Mirabel restaurant and will be there promptly at 12:30. You will have no trouble recognizing me. I am quite tall and will be wearing a flowered frock and a large white hat with white lilacs on it. Impatiently

Your grandmother

P.S. The Mirabel is quite near the hotel. The porter can show you the way.

The white hat with the lilacs made me think suddenly of my grandfather saying "people stood on chairs to look at her at races and public functions."

I wondered what it would be like to be as beautiful as that. But inside I went both hot and cold, one minute filled with impatience to see her, the next filled with an overwhelming desire to run away altogether.

I had a bath and put on my best suit, one of the four my grandfather had ordered in Boston for the trip. All four had long trousers, the first I had ever had for although I was a year or two younger than the other boys I was big for my age and bigger than most of them. I had the same slim, wiry build of my grandfather with very dark hair and eyes like his. I dressed very carefully and neatly and even sprinkled my handkerchief with eau-de-cologne which I borrowed from one of the boys. I was going to lunch not only with my grandmother but with a great beauty and a great woman of the world.

The porter gave me directions, which were simple enough, I could have found the place after a block or two simply by following the sound of the music. It was a lovely day such as one finds in summer in the Tyrol and the Salzkammergut with a brilliant sun and a cool breeze from the mountains and forests. The old pink and yellow and grey baroque houses, built against the sidewalks, with the gardens behind, were mottled by the shadows of the trees. Then I turned the corner and there beneath a grove of linden trees was the restaurant with tables all set in the shade and a little orchestra already playing waltzes and polkas for the people having *apéritifs*. Beyond the restaurant itself lay the Mirabelgarten with its beds of flowers, its white balustrades and rows of gay and fantastic baroque statues set against the greenery. One saw the sun-drenched spaces of the Mirabelgarten across and beyond the deep shade which the linden trees cast over the little tables.

Because I was nervous I was early and sat at a table waiting for my grandmother to arrive, ordering a beer with the manner of a great man of the world, thinking what a long way this all was from the Valley. I had begun really to enjoy myself and the whole of the Grand Tour. When I look back now, I must have been a source of amusement to the waiter and to some of the worldly people at the neighboring tables—a rather gawky boy, fourteen years old, dressed in the most American of clothes and wearing a flat hat of straw adorned with the school ribbon. But I think that the occasion marked one more small but significant step in my becoming a man, for it was the first time I had ever thought of myself in that way or certainly the first time I had ever suspected the immense pleasure of going out alone and independently, seeking adventure.

People came and went to and from the bright tables all about me—fashionably dressed baronesses and actresses and pretty women in the dirndls of the countryside, mustachioed men with beards or muttonchop whiskers or officers in the bright uniforms of the gay and tragic old empire. As I drank my beer, in as worldly a manner as possible, I felt myself slipping imperceptibly into the picture, becoming a part of it, savoring the flavor of it as one savors the flavor of good wine and deciding for myself, without even knowing it at the time, that this was an extremely pleasant and agreeable life which I would enjoy more and more deeply as I grew older. I even pictured myself a few years hence spending a summer in this or some other European watering place, with a pretty actress as a mistress.

I had no scruples of morality and not the vestige of Puritanism for in my strange upbringing, even in the heart of the Middle West, there had never been any of the Calvinist fears or pressures which corrupted and deformed the lives of so many other boys. My grandfather had never been a church-goer and secretly held a contempt for church hierarchies and theology. He was a deeply religious man but his religion had nothing whatever to do with priests or churches. I have never known a better citizen nor a more kindly man. His morality was founded rather upon ethics than upon ecclesiastical dogma. He had a simple but generous and all-encompassing rule of behavior—that one must

173

never consciously be guilty of an act which will hurt or damage another person or damage or threaten the structure or stability of human society. That was his code. His religious sense, like that of the eighteenth century mystics and philosophers was deep and sincere and found expression in all the manifestations of nature. I have thought sometimes that he believed even trees had souls. I am certain he believed in the souls of animals and birds. Once I heard him say to Aunt Susan, rather impatiently. "Of course churches are necessary. They are necessary refuges for those who are ignorant or afraid—which is most of the human race. And they help to keep that element in order. Without organized religion we should have chaos because most of the human race has not reached that stage where the individual has the courage and the intelligence to accept the universe as it is and what is more important to find delight in it and behave himself." The speech was remarkable coming from a man who had been hurt many times in his life by the acts of others and in particular by the wife whom he had worshipped and whom at that moment I was waiting to see for the first time.

All this had a great deal to do with the boy sitting at the table in the Mirabelgarten. The thoughts he had when he pictured himself spending a happy summer with a pretty mistress were not lascivious

or evil or suppressed as the thoughts of a Calvinist boy might be (thinking of the legs beneath
the long trailing skirts), but were merely gay and
natural thoughts. Such an adventure would be fun,
as indeed it proved to be more than ten years later.
There were certain things in life which already I
knew I must never do, certain acts which were evil
because they injured others. But for the rest, the
already projected summer excursion with the
actress for example, was a part of the happy natural
order of things.

Sitting thus under the trees I was growing up,
and very rapidly too in that hour I waited for my
grandmother to arrive and in the hour or two which
followed. It was for this that my grandfather had
sent me on the Grand Tour.

The truth of course was that I was daydreaming in the midst of all these people with the
orchestra playing waltzes almost in my ears, daydreaming as completely as I might have been alone
on the ledge high above the swamp in the Wild
Country which I had discovered that uneasy day
with Wayne. So far gone was I that I wakened
with a start when just below me on the opposite
side of the balustrade a white hat with lilacs swam
into my vision.

Just below me with her back to me was my grandmother in the hat and the flowered dress she had
described. With her was a man wearing dark

glasses. She carried a lacy parasol over her shoulder and was giving instructions to the elderly, bearded driver of a Victoria. As she talked to him she twirled the parasol gently and this movement, together with the sound of a rather deep and musical voice, gave me an irresistible impression of gaiety which eased a little my sense of awkwardness and tension. I rose quickly from my table and went down the short flight of stairs. I reached her just as she finished her directions to the driver and turned away from him. I was carrying the ridiculous straw boater with my school colors in my hand and as our eyes met the light of recognition came into her face. She said, "Ronnie!" And before I knew what had happened she kissed me lightly and quickly on the cheek. The action was so spontaneous, so gay and so deft that all sense of strangeness was banished. It was as if I already knew her well and we were meeting after a short absence.

"I'm afraid I'm a little late. We drove out to the Bishop's Palace and didn't allow enough time."

Then before I could answer she turned to the man at her side and said, "Here he is, René. . . . But what a big boy!" And to me she said, "This is my friend, René Chastel."

He held out his hand vaguely in my direction and I saw that he was quite blind and realized that this was the man who had long ago caused my

176

grandfather's great unhappiness. I could not have any resentment toward him for what happened since so much time lay in between, but if there had been any awkwardness it would have been swept away quickly by the gesture with which she somehow managed to envelop the three of us, drawing us together. It was as if she had swept away in a single manifestation of her charm any stiffness or formality there might have been. The truth was that I fell in love with my grandmother on sight, which was exactly what she had meant me to do.

With her blind companion on one side, clinging lightly to her arm and with me on the other she led us toward the stairway and at sight of us the proprietor, a big man with Franz Josef whiskers came quickly down and said in German, "Madame! What a pleasure! We have your table. When we received your order this morning and heard you were back, the whole place was changed."

She laughed and told him in perfect German not to be so flattering—that she knew the ways of proprietors. And then held out her hand, which he kissed with the most elaborate bow.

It was a table at the edge of the little terrace overlooking the tables under the trees with the view of the gay Mirabelgarten just beyond.

She had ordered the luncheon and the wine in advance so there was no scrambling over a menu card and now for the first time with the first awkwardness and bedazzlement past, I really saw her.

She had the tall, straight carriage of a girl of twenty, although she was well over sixty at the time, and her face was almost unlined beneath the discreet make-up which had been put on with great skill. She was really neither old nor young in appearance nor did she have that dreadful quality described as "well preserved." Her features were large but finely cut with delicate eyebrows which arched above eyes which seemed violet but changeable in the shifting sunlight and shadow. Her hair was quite white and that perhaps made her face seem younger. The collar of the dress she wore rose high about her long throat with stiff wired points just beneath the small, pretty ears which were exposed by the upswept fashion in which she wore her hair.

She had that size and carriage which is usually inseparable from the quality of those women of her time who were almost professional beauties. It is difficult for small women to attain the quality of beauty, however pretty they may be, for beauty, I think, implies a certain stature and dignity. Now as an old lady, after a long life in which she had received perpetually the tributes and respect given to beauty, she had come to have a charming time-lessness, as if beauty alone were enough to win for her favor and admiration. The impervious, indestructible quality was there in the way she carried herself, the way she sat. It was in the tilt of her head and in the grace with which she accepted the low bow and hand-kissing of the proprietor. But what astonished me most, I think, was her quality of happiness and adjustment to everything about her—to the beauty of the day, to the sunlight, to the mingled ordeal and pleasure of meeting a grandson, nearly grown, whom she had never seen before, even to the tragedy of the blindness which had fallen upon her companion. Here, sitting opposite me, was no suffering or soured or repentant sinner. It was as if everything about her, the frivolous parasol, the humorous sparkle of the eye, the neat, chic white gloves, the gay lilacs on the huge hat, the curve of her lips when she smiled all proclaimed that this was a good world and a good life whatever its sorrows and complexities.

It was clear that her companion felt an adoration of her, even after nearly thirty years. As she talked he kept turning his sightless eyes toward her as if he were still able to enjoy through the sense of vision the sparkle of her young eyes, the curve of the lips and the little gestures she made with her small, pretty hands and, it is possible that having known her so well and for so long, he was able in his imagination to reconstruct these things so that through the sound of her voice and her laugh alone he actually did *see* her.

I do not know his age but it must have been about the same as my grandmother's. It did not matter much for he was a handsome man with that beautifully sculptured face, very clean and classical in its outlines, which one finds sometimes among Latins. Although his hair was quite grey, it was clear that it must have been black for his skin was very dark. Now it had the yellowish tinge of the skin of one who was desperately ill with an illness which could not be cured. His hands were large and strong, but at the same time beautiful and sensitive—hands which a palmist would call those of a passionate lover. A generation earlier they must have been a singularly handsome couple and even a generation later when they were both dead and I was grown and married with a son of my own, I still heard older people in Rome and Florence and Paris talk of them as if, already, they had become a legend. They never had a great deal of money. My grandmother had a little of her own and Chastel belonged to a sugar family in France and had an income which varied. He also had a tiny income that came out of articles he wrote about pictures and music. In these fields he had a considerable reputation as a critic.

Years afterward I discovered from my Aunt Susan that my grandfather had offered to make my grandmother a yearly allowance but that she had refused it. He must have loved her very much indeed.

We had a lunch of *hors d'oeuvre*, Salzburger nockerl (a speciality of the establishment), a wonderful Wiener Schnitzel, a salad and fresh fruit. With each course, my grandmother took over quietly arranging the food for her companion, so quietly and so unobtrusively that I scarcely noticed what she was doing. He had not been blind for long and had not yet acquired the skill with which people long blind manage the smaller hardships of their condition.

I remember very little of the conversation on that day and I realize now that this was because nothing very important was said. My grandmother was not a brilliant conversationalist. It was not her mind or its cleverness which made her attractive but rather her manner and her power of making you seem the brilliant and interesting one in any conversation. This is a very great art indeed which has rather grown out of fashion and should not be undervalued. Hardly one woman in a thousand understands it today. It is a pity because nothing makes a woman more attractive or gives her greater power and authority. It was, of course, the secret of women like Pompadour and even of Maintenon who had been a governess and was already a middle-aged woman when she acquired her ascendancy over Louis XIV. As I heard my grandfather once say, "It is impossible to spend twenty-four hours a day in bed. No woman has ever held a man by that power alone." And I knew then that what my grandfather had missed through all the years of separation was not simply the beauty of Melissa but her power of making a room or a day or an occasion seem more brilliant and pleasing than it really was, or perhaps it was that she acted merely as a catalytic agent which brought into reality all the delightful potentialities of an incident or an occasion.

I know that she managed that day to dissipate, quickly and completely, all the shyness which for me was inevitable in such a meeting and the awkwardness which is inevitably a characteristic of any boy of fourteen who is not a prig and unbearably precocious. Before we had finished the nockerl, we were old friends. But more extraordinary was the fact that she had brought myself, an awkward, unworldly country boy and Chastel, one of the most civilized and worldly of Frenchmen, together upon a basis of friendship and common interests.

This would have seemed virtually impossible if she had not chosen the Valley of all places as the base from which to carry out her campaign. Of course she had lived there in summer as a bride and as a young woman and she had always been a great horsewoman so she knew every back road and lane and even some of the more open deer trails in the Wild Country. It was remarkable how many trails of conversation and interest she discovered which began in the Valley and led outward into the great world, into art and music and history and many other fields. She managed at once to bring Chastel into the Valley, into *my* world, and to take me out of it into the great world which such a man knew so well. There were, of course, the trotting races and the horses about which he knew a great deal for trotting races were very popular in Italy and there was always the European Hambletonian held each year at Vincennes near Paris. And the Wild Country in the evening was like the pictures of Claude Lorrain and at different seasons and under varying atmospheric conditions like the landscapes of Constable. And we talked of the wonderful *blue* light in the evenings which I had always taken for granted as commonplace until I had gone out into the world and discovered that only certain conditions of atmospheric moisture and crops and forest and temperature produced that strange, luminous beauty which at sunset turned all blue flowers like the spires of delphinium, phosphorescent and ringed by a cold, blue fire.

And she talked of the wild, hot beauty of the music made by the Negroes from the cabins in the summer evenings and of their shuffling sometimes orgiastic dancing, and of the characters which hill country like that at Clarendon inevitably produces everywhere in the world. Many of them she knew were dead for they were already old people when she was young, but I told her of the whole new crop which had come up like Old Virgil and Mattie and Red who loved both horses and women with such passion. And Chastel took a great interest in the Indian history of the Valley so strange and exotic to him and so familiar and commonplace to me. I found myself, to my own astonishment, telling him familiar legends, such as the death of the squaw and her baby who had thrown herself and the baby from the high rock behind the house in Clarendon to escape a troup of scouting whites, and of the Benson family massacre on the farm where Henry and Vinnie lived. And I told him about the French blood which had come down through my grandfather to me from the early French settlers in the vast reaches of the Louisiana territory.

I knew that Chastel enjoyed all the talk for it brought fresh interest to his civilized, tired, cynical mind. As for myself, I felt myself growing in mind and spirit as clearly as I'd felt the physical "growing pains" during the hot, restless nights at Clarendon, when my boy's body was changing into the body of a man.

I know too that all my interest in pictures and

painters began on that bright, gay day at the Mirabelgarten where we talked of light and technique and landscapes. Until that moment all the pictures we had seen under the able guidance of Mr. Pulsifer while trudging through the great galleries of Europe had meant little to me unless they touched upon some literary or historical event in which I was interested. On that day I discovered that painting in itself could be a subject of the greatest interest and lend a fascination to the plainest, simplest painting of a pitcher, a few apples and a dish. As I sat there I resolved to revisit the Louvre when I returned to Paris and go expressly to look at the luminous landscapes of Claude Lorrain which reproduced so beautifully, according to my grandmother, the light and the tree shapes of our own familiar Valley in Missouri. I went there a week later and found suddenly that what had once seemed to me dull and ancient paintings, had become alive and new and filled with fascination.

It was then that I understood for the first time with real clarity what my grandfather had wanted to do for me in sending me on the Grand Tour. He had wanted to create for me the treasury of knowledge and appreciation and interest by which civilized people live, that treasury which served as a bulwark against the disappointments and disillusionment of daily living. It was that which had made possible his acceptance and perhaps even his understanding and forgiveness of what my grandmother had done. It was that treasury and bulwark which made the difference between the richness of a life like his and the bare misery and poverty of a life like Old Virgil's. There was another richness, equally important, which he knew well enough he had already given me—that infinite richness founded upon a love and knowledge and understanding of all that had to do with nature. He knew how deeply I loved the whole of the Valley and that I could go off alone all day among its streams and hills and woods, content and all unlonely in the exploration of new delights and the confirmation of old and familiar ones. That treasury no one could ever destroy or dissipate, for in essence it was utterly indestructible and could not be lost as wealth or even reputation may be. It was for this he had approved and encouraged my friendship with Henry, and oddly enough on that day in far-off Salzburg I thought more than once of Henry who might have been bewildered by so much of our talk.

But he had wanted me to know as well the delights of the mind and of art and of pure thought and all the values and beauty which go with these things and are unknown to those not fortunate enough to have acquired them. They too were indestructible. I understood why it was that above his desk in the shuttered library at Clarendon there stood a plaster bust of Voltaire by Houdon. More than any other man in all history, Voltaire had known the delights alike of the mind, of the senses, and of nature. Like my grandfather, Voltaire had separated religion from behavior and had kept his mysticism apart as the truest manifestation of the religious spirit. I learned on that first voyage into Europe much that my grandfather had wanted me to learn and that he knew he could never explain to me, for the treasure he sought to disclose to me could not be explained or described to those who have never discovered it. One can put the key into the hand of the novice but he must himself open the door and explore more and more deeply the endless and glittering corners in which the treasure lies hidden.

All this he had managed to do for me, not unaided, for in my occasional homesickness for the Valley I had often been bored and impatient to return. His greatest confederate in the plot turned out to be my grandmother and whether he knew or suspected this I cannot say, although out of his intimate knowledge of her he must have believed in her power to help both him and me in what he was trying to achieve.

Whatever the truth, it was my grandmother in those brief two or three hours in the Mirabelgarten who gave me the key to the delights which have never ceased to increase and which, together with those of nature, have armored me for all my life against the toughest and most painful assaults of chance and fortune and tragedy. That they are indestructible is their greatest virtue and value.

While we sat there, she and Chastel managed somehow to concentrate a great many glories into a very small space, much as a magnifying glass concentrates the immeasurable heat and light of the sun within a tiny circle. They had managed to change everything for me so that even the Valley, which I knew better than anything in life, had become a different place, capable of delights and satisfactions which had until now gone unnoticed and unobserved.

At a little after three, my grandmother said, "We shall have to leave, Ronnie, for we must not miss the last train to Bad Gastein. I've sent the bags to the station so we have only to drive there with no time wasted."

The Victoria with the bearded old driver was waiting for us and I sat on the small seat opposite the two of them on our drive to the station. We had only a few minutes before the train left and my last glimpse of them was of my grandmother helping Chastel gently into one of the old-fashioned compartments. As the train left she leaned out to wave to me and with a kind of ache in my heart, I waved back to her. And then she was gone.

I did not know then that I would see her again much sooner than I had believed, for as the train drew out of sight in the direction of the mountains my only thought was that I might never see her again. I did not know then that Chastel had only a little time to live and that it was necessary for him to return that same night because he was so ill. Nor did I know that, whatever she might be suffering at the knowledge, she was resolved never to betray her feelings but only to make the days or perhaps the hours which remained for him to live, as painless and as pleasant as was possible. She had meant me to fall in love with her and she had succeeded. I think her aim in life was always to be pleasing and that is a great aim for any woman and one which gives her a power which is perhaps greater than any other a woman can achieve. In her case I think it atoned for whatever wrong she had been guilty of toward my grandfather. I am sure now that she could not have helped herself and that if she had attempted to do so, she might only have brought greater unhappiness to herself and to him and lost that power of making the world seem an infinitely brighter and more charming place for all those who knew her. Unlike many great beauties she did not consider it enough merely to be beautiful and to take selfishly those rewards which are given freely to beauty itself by a hungry world. She had not the shallow egotism of most beauties. I think that these are the reasons why, unlike most beauties, she survived and was beautiful and was ageless as a woman of sixty-five. She had no need for the artifices or the hardships which some women, whose only resource is physical beauty, endure as they grow older in order to preserve what cannot be preserved and so turn weary and bitter and raddled. She was pleasing. I think that would be in itself and alone a great epitaph for any woman.

PART IV

AS WAS PLANNED, WE SAILED HOME FROM
Liverpool on the old *Celtic* and I took the train from
New York on the evening of landing as my grandfather had arranged. It was an impatient trip in
which the train seemed to crawl all the way for the
time left at Clarendon before the opening of school
was all too brief. On the second night I scarcely
slept at all and was up at daylight to watch from
the train window the rich, green country through
which we passed and which I loved so much.

My grandfather was waiting in the new station
at St. Louis and, guessing how I felt, had arranged
to take the first train out of St. Louis for Masonville and the Valley. He looked at me and said,
"Well, son, you've grown. I wouldn't have thought
it possible." But it was true. Even the sleeves of
my new suits were already growing a little short.

On the train I asked him for news of Clarendon
but there wasn't any. The horses were doing well
on the Grand Circuit though my grandfather had

gone to only two or three meetings. Although he did not admit it, I gathered that as he grew older he found the heat of the rich middle-western summer and the life in hotels had become too tiring for him.

He asked me about the trip, rather tentatively at first but as I talked of all I had done he seemed to grow excited and younger and I could see that he would like to visit Paris and Rome and all the other places he had known so well and to which he had not returned since my grandmother had left him. I felt shy about speaking of her although, as I know now, that was what he wanted more than anything else. In the end he was forced to speak of the meeting. He tried to do it casually saying, "And your grandmother? Did that come off all right?"

"It was wonderful," I said, "I liked her very much." And I tried as well as an inarticulate boy of fourteen could, to tell him about the meeting.

As I talked his eyes brightened and now and then he said, "Yes, that's very like her!" or "Yes, that's just what she would have done!" And he even chuckled once or twice. Very slowly I came to understand that he was still in love with her. When I tried to explain to him how interesting the conversation had been, he said, "Yes, she's a very clever and brilliant woman although she has a horror of anyone discovering it." Then he added, "That was it! That's what I wanted you to see—

that there was much more to the world than the Valley and your school." And I could see that he was pleased.

Then casually he said, "I forgot to tell you. Wayne is staying with us for a week or two. It seems he'll be elected all right."

And suddenly a sense of depression clouded the joy over my return. I wished that he hadn't been there. When I tried to discover why I felt that way, I could find no more tangible answer than I had found on the day the feeling first came over me. It had something to do with his voice, the way he rumpled my hair, the way he had breathed as we watched the breeding of the young mare.

Aunt Susan had driven in to meet us at Mason-ville, looking as fresh and brisk and wrenlike as always. Wayne, she said, would have met us but he went off on a long walk and hadn't come back in time so when Jasper brought the buggy around she had just taken the reins and driven in town.

As we passed Old Virgil's place on the way to the farm, the Kleinfelter girl was in the yard and waved to us and Aunt Susan said, "I hear Mattie isn't so well. It would be a mercy if she just died in her sleep. Doc tells me that she's simply falling apart—that nothing functions any more." Then after a silence, she said, "It's a wonder to me some-times why a person like Mattie was ever born. For the last twenty years she can't have had any pleasure except the awful one of keeping Virgil miserable —and that could hardly be a pleasure."

"I guess it's about even between them," observed my grandfather.

"He's been telling gossip around the Valley again about Vinnie and he talks against Henry all the time. He says Henry is nothing but a fool and that the new-fangled ideas he's trying will bankrupt him. He says nobody but a fool would marry a woman like Vinnie."

"What's the matter with Vinnie?" I asked.

"Nothing's the matter!" said Aunt Susan.

"Then why does he talk that way about them? They've never done him any harm."

It was my grandfather who answered me. He said, "Son, it's because Henry and Vinnie have got everything that Virgil's never had and never will have now. Of all the sins, envy and the bitterness that goes with it are the blackest." He looked at me and added, "That's something to remember now and always. It isn't only wicked because of the direct evil it can cause but because it destroys the one who envies. It's like acid eating away inside you." He sighed and spoke again, "But I suppose Virgil's never really had a chance. His father wouldn't let him go to school after the fourth grade. He took him out and made him work on the farm. He was the ugly kind who believed that hard work, however stupid, is an all-healing virtue.

Virgil's got the same idea. Virgil never knew much. He hates his own land. He wrestles with his own farm in a passion of hatred for it . . . and he never had the gumption to leave it, and find something else he needn't hate."

As we drove up I heard Wayne's voice call out to us. Turning toward the sound I discovered him looking out of the window of the bathroom on the second floor. He was standing there, wrapped in a towel, his hair wet and rumpled.

"Hello, Ronnie!" he called out, "Welcome home!" And again the uneasiness came over me. Then he called out, "I'll be right down!" and disappeared from the window.

I heard my grandfather chuckling as he observed, "It must be terrible to feel as healthy as Wayne always does. It's almost a disease to be as vigorous as that."

Then Prince ran down the steps and drive to meet us barking all the way from the house to the carriage. He looked heavier than when I left him and my grandfather said, "He's showing his age. He must be nearly thirteen years old. You were about two when Henry's father brought him over as a pup."

Jasper, who had been watching for us as we came across the Valley, came to take the horses and said, "Well, Mr. Ronnie, you're getting real grown-up with them long pants on."

It was too late to go anywhere before dinner so I unpacked my bags and had a bath, stopping now and then to look out of the window down the Valley toward the Wild Country. It was lovely in the changing light, and I was glad to be back. The only jarring note in my pleasure was the reek of the eau-de-cologne Wayne had used after his bath. And it wasn't only the eau-de-cologne; it seemed to me that there was another odor, of fleshliness, of something I had not been aware of before.

I wanted to go off tomorrow early into the Wild Country, but I did not want him to go with me and spoil the trip. I would have to shake him off somehow.

When I came down at the sound of the first bell for dinner my grandfather and Wayne were already on the big verandah having juleps. Wayne said, "Well, boy, I suppose you're glad to be back?" He held out his hand and when I went over to take it he caught me in the vice of his big knees and made the old gesture of rumpling my hair. I had hoped that in the dignity of my long trousers it would not happen and when I felt the heat of his big thighs against my legs, I was overcome by a sudden fury and struck him on the shoulders, pushing him away and saying, "Don't do that! Please!"

There was a moment of awkwardness and I saw

the look of surprise on my grandfather's face. I knew that my own face was scarlet and suddenly I was ashamed of my rudeness when I heard my grandfather saying, "He's getting to be grown-up, Wayne. You know how it is with your first long pants."

Wayne laughed and said, "Sure, *I* know!" But his eyes had a curious look, as if the pupils had contracted like the eyes of a cat in a strong light.

The sudden, confused, blaze of quick anger left me feeling tired and limp, and all through dinner I could find nothing to say except when I was asked a question, yet I felt a certain satisfaction for I was sure that Wayne would not annoy me again by touching me. Somehow the flash of anger had cleared the air between us.

After dinner I went out to the stables and there to my surprise I found Red who I thought was away with the horses on the Circuit. He was standing outside the stable which in winter housed the brood mares, his bow legs arched, his thick muscular body held a little back as if bracing himself. He was very tanned from the summer's racing and seemed glad to see me.

He said, "We missed you, kid!"

I asked him how the horses were doing and he said, "Fine! We've won three out of five races this summer. A stable can't hope to do better than that."

I told him what Chastel had said of the trotting races in Europe which I had not known existed and he said, "Sure. We've sold some mares over there. I'd like to go over sometime and see for myself. Travel, they say, is an education in itself. How did you get on with the lingo?"

"Pretty good." And then out of the gathering twilight, Wayne appeared from the direction of the Big House. It seemed that he and Red hadn't seen each other for a couple of months and there was a big show of greeting. Then Wayne laughed and asked, "Had pretty good huntin' this summer?"

Red grinned and took the toothpick from between his teeth. "Sure! I never had a better season. There was a redheaded girl went along with me all the way east to Goshen. She was all right!"

"I always kind of favored redheads. Two redheads together must have been pretty hot," said Wayne. "I remember back, three winters ago at the state capital, I had a redhead off and on all winter. She couldn't get enough. She was married but her husband was away most of the time on the road. But she liked it so much she'd manage to sneak away even when he was home."

Red chuckled, as if thinking back over his countless conquests, and I managed to ease my way along the stables pretending to look at a couple of late foals while they went on talking, comparing amorous experiences and techniques in the frankest of language. It wasn't that I was priggish. I didn't care if they wanted to talk thus and enjoyed it. In my inexperience I was embarrassed and I was surprised to hear Wayne talking in the same language and with the same zest as Red. You expected it of Red, but Wayne was a lawyer and an educated man was different. I was certain that his coarseness would have astonished my grandfather.

I managed to slip out of the stable and was walking toward the Big House when Wayne caught up with me.

"What are you doing tomorrow? I suppose you'll be going down to the Wild Country?"

I resolved then to lie to him since it seemed the only way out. "No," I said, "I think I'll go for a walk about the farm and go over to see Henry in the afternoon."

The plan formed itself suddenly in my mind. I'd follow the creek down into the Big Swamp, taking my lunch with me and stop at Henry's and Vinnie's on my way back. I knew I'd be tired by then and that Henry would drive me back.

"I've got some work to do," said Wayne, "and I think I'll do some riding in the afternoon. I'll try out that new mare. Your grandfather says she needs some exercise. We can go to the Wild Country some other day. That suit you?"

"Yes, that will be fine."

It surprised me that he thought it a pleasure to me to have him go with me, but perhaps I was wrong to have been surprised. Until this summer it had always been a treat.

Then quietly he asked, "What made you jump at me this afternoon? You know, there on the verandah."

I felt the color rising in my face and was glad for the gathering darkness. I said, "I don't know. Something bit me, I guess. I'm sorry."

He laughed, "There's nothing to be sorry about. I was your age myself once. Everything is kind of mixed up. It'll straighten out later. Don't worry too much about it."

"I'm not worrying," I said sullenly. I was angry again this time because he was patronizing me.

"You're a good lookin' kid," he said. "If you play your cards right when you grow up you can have anything you want."

I didn't know what he meant—whether it was friends or money, or success, or power, or women but I think now that he meant all of those things for he always used his own good looks, brains and physique and personality unscrupulously to win for him whatever he wanted at the moment. However much I disliked him then or however much I dislike the memory of him today, it was true that he had all these things. He was a very beautiful male whore. I know that on that short walk from the stables to the house I had a feeling that I was being corrupted and I am certain now that his intention was a perverse one of corruption, slow and insidious. I do not know why this was so, unless there was in him a desire to bring others to his own level of sensuality and indulgence. There are many people in the world like that, both men and women. I know now that it was the awareness of this corruption which, unrecognized and misunderstood, had changed everything between us. I had not noticed it before perhaps because I was too young or more likely because it was only as I began to grow up that the possibility of my corruption presented itself to him. Why he embarked upon such a course unless it was the one he followed with everyone, or what it was he intended, I do not know to this day.

We were suddenly climbing the steps of the verandah where my grandfather and Aunt Susan were sitting in the darkness. I bade them good night for I was tired from the sleeplessness and exhaustion of the journey home. After I had gone to bed I thought for a while about my grandmother, seeing her very clearly as she waved to me out of the window of the departing train, and I thought of Henry and Vinnie and the baby that was named for me. Aunt Susan had said there would be a regular christening with me standing up as Godfather, and again I felt an overwhelming love for the three of them as if somehow I were a part of the love and the happiness they represented.

I heard the distant hooting of an owl and a distant rumble of thunder from the head of the Valley and then I fell asleep. Once during the night the sound of the wild storm wakened me but I fell asleep again almost at once.

I left the house a little after sunrise with Prince, my rifle and a lunch which old Jackson had packed for me the night before. The early departure was part of the plot for it allowed no possibility of Wayne's changing his mind and joining me.

After the thunderstorm the morning was cool and brilliant with the air washed clean and the moisture dripping from the trees. Prince, older and heavier, behaved like a puppy, running and barking and jumping against me.

We took the familiar course across the mint-covered bluegrass meadow to the marsh-bordered creek. We had all day before us so we did not hurry but went slowly, stopping at pools to watch the fish in the clear water and exploring deep in the thickets which bordered the stream. Once or twice without success I had a pot shot at a crow which I knew I could not hit and had no real desire to hit. There was little of the killer in me and for that I think Henry was responsible. In all our ramblings before he married Vinnie, he would always prefer to lie quite still to watch a bird or an animal rather than to kill it.

It was nearly noon when we crossed the country road that separated Henry's farm from the Wild Country and there we left the creek for the deer trail which Wayne and I had discovered on the earlier visit. It was my plan to follow the trail deep into the swamps for the going was easier than following the bed of the stream and I could penetrate more deeply into the thicket in much less time. I planned to return to the limestone ridge and eat my lunch on the peak of the grassy shelf overlooking the whole county. After that I would follow the deer trail back to the county road and from there go to visit Henry and Vinnie.

I was still young enough to put drama and imagination into such an excursion and now as I advanced, I became Doctor Livingstone lost in the swamps of the Nyanza. It was an easy role for the setting was all there—a luxuriant swamp thickly overgrown with reeds and elders and ferns and tangled by a luxuriant growth of wild grapevines. Without the neatly broken deer trail which in places simply became a dark, cool tunnel, dripping with the rain of the night before, I would have made little headway. Old Prince was tired out by now and plodded silently at my heels scarcely troubling to sniff at the scent of the wild animals which here and there crossed the trail.

It was noon when we reached the edges of the lake which had been my goal. It was about here, I thought, that Doctor Stanley would have found me. But there was no way of reaching the lake for the deer trail turned away sharply leading into still thicker jungle, and between me and the lake lay a wide swamp thickly overgrown with cattails, water lilies and bulrushes. I was hungry by now but strong-willed enough to maintain my determination to return to the high ridge. The midges and mosquitoes served to strengthen my resolution for they had become numerous and voracious.

Turning back, we reached the foot of the ridge a little before one o'clock and began the steep, rough climb. Twice on the way up I waited for old Prince to ease his panting and get his breath. It took us nearly ten minutes to reach the ledge with its carpet of wild flowers and as I climbed over the edge I made a startling discovery. The wild flowers had been beaten down over a small area as if someone had been resting or sleeping there quite recently. For a moment I stepped out of the role of Doctor Livingstone and became Robinson Crusoe at the moment he came upon the footprint in the sand. And then I remembered the cheap woman's handkerchief which Wayne and I had found there the year before.

Someone knew this ledge—someone who lived in the neighborhood and came here. They must have come for some special reason for it was a long way from the road and the climb up to it was steep and difficult. Even now whoever it was might be near at hand, perhaps watching me out of the thick undergrowth below.

For a moment I considered throwing myself down on the thick turf and then abandoned the idea. The view would be finer from the summit of the little peak that rose twenty or thirty feet above the ridge. So Prince and I climbed the remaining distance and found at the top of the little peak a shady place in the shadow of the outcropping rock. There we sat and I opened the lunch and began sharing it with the old dog.

Old Jackson had done well. There were sandwiches both of chicken and cold beef, pickles and olives and a great piece of chocolate cake encrusted thickly with maple icing which had grown a little soggy on the journey, a condition which did not deter the voracious appetite of a growing boy.

I had been right about the view. The ten or twenty feet difference in altitude enlarged enormously the whole aspect of the Wild Country. Immediately below us lay a flat sea of deep-green jungly vegetation with here and there a great virgin oak rising from a dry knob that emerged above the level of the swamp. Beyond lay the expanse of brilliant blue water glittering now in the brilliance of the midday August sun. And still further lay the hills, one after another, fading away into a translucent blue haze. But to me it was not the same landscape which I had seen the year before from the same ridge. At least, I saw it quite differently now. I saw it as it might have been painted by Constable or Claude Lorrain. I noticed beauties in it I had not seen before—beauties of light and shadow, of tone and value and composition which before had remained hidden or obscured to a sensibility which had reacted to romantic nature alone. I thought how greatly Lorrain or Constable would have enjoyed painting the whole scene with the deep-blue shadows of the great cottony cloud overhead scudding across the distant lake and the sea of deep-green foliage just below. But for my grandmother and those few hours spent with her in distant Austria I would have seen none of these things. And I thought suddenly how wonderful it would be to be a great painter who could paint such a scene and reveal these beauties to others whose eyes unaided could not discover them.

I sat there dreaming as I ate and in a little time nothing remained of the lunch and old Prince was licking up the crumbs from the waxed paper in which it had been wrapped. When no crumbs remained, both Prince and I were seized with the same idea—a nap. In the pocket in the rock the green plants made a soft bed. I lay down and Prince curled himself into a ball with his head resting on my knee. Then we both fell asleep.

I must have slept for nearly an hour and I wakened slowly and reluctantly in a haze of sensuous comfort. First I noticed that Prince in the heat had moved away from me and was lying with his head between his paws watching me and then I heard the faint sound of voices. The old dog showed no sign of alarm. He did not bark and the hair did not rise on his back. At first I thought that in his growing deafness he had not heard the voices but almost at once I understood why he showed no interest. It was because, with his sharp senses, he *knew* the voices and then I knew them too.

They were the voices of Wayne Torrance and of Vinnie!

With the sense of recognition came a sense of bewilderment and of shock and instinctively I reached over to place my hand on the old dog's head to keep him quiet. I did so not out of any desire to eavesdrop but because I knew that something wrong was going on a little way from us, that I could not stop it and that I must not be discovered. Suddenly awake and alert I understood clearly what the two voices were saying. I might

207

have thrust my fingers in my ears but I was power-less to do so.

I heard Wayne's voice saying, "What difference can it make to anyone? No one will ever know. It means so much to me and it is such a little thing. It can hurt no one."

There was a silence and then Vinnie's voice with its faint accent, "But it isn't like that. It is bad, for me! Don't you see?"

And Wayne's voice again, a voice I had never heard, low and husky, both pleading and com-manding. It was like the laying on of hands. There was a quality in it which frightened me by its urgency and concentrated desire. "You haven't forgotten what it was like . . . remember Vinnie? . . . It can't hurt anyone. Not this once . . . remem-ber what it was like?"

And wildly I heard Vinnie say, "No! No! Don't do that! Don't touch me! Wayne, don't touch me!"

Then there was a silence in which I could hear Wayne's heavy breathing that was almost like sobbing.

Then Vinnie said, "No . . . No . . . Please don't touch me. Please! For God's sake, No!" And then the voice trailed off into silence.

For a long time I heard nothing at all but I dared not look to see whether they were gone lest they were still there and would discover me. Now the horror of such a possibility I could not face.

And after a long time I heard the sound of hysterical sobbing that came unmistakably from Vinnie, and Wayne's voice, "Don't take it like that! What does it matter? We're only alive once. What has happened is the greatest thing in the world. Don't you see, Vinnie? We're lucky! Don't you see how lucky we are?" He spoke still in a low, quiet voice. It was that corruption working again, less subtle and more urgent than the corruption with which he had slowly tried to surround me and more dangerous too.

The sobbing went on and then Vinnie said, "I ought to kill myself . . . if I wasn't a coward. I ought to kill myself! That's what I ought to do." And then almost shrilly she cried out, "Don't do that! Don't touch me, you devil! Haven't you done enough? Let me alone!"

Then came a faint rustling sound and I heard Wayne say, "You're not going back yet . . . not now. It can't make any difference now! You can't go away and leave now. We may never be together again." There was the sound of something desperate and urgent in the voice.

"I am going back. Let me alone! If you don't let me alone . . . if you ever bother me again, I'll get a gun and kill you! I'll kill you! You hear me, Wayne? I'll kill you! Let me go! Don't touch me."

Then Wayne's voice with a new note in it, a

209

note of wild, insane fury. "You're not going! You hear me! You're not going!"

"I'll kill you! I swear I'll kill you!"

Then came the sound of fists striking against flesh, pummeling it and then a thudding sound followed by a faint, hysterical sobbing and the rattle of a dislodged rock as it fell down the side of the ridge. And then nothing at all.

For a long time I waited, every nerve tense with listening and when there was only silence for a long period, I crawled cautiously out of the pocket in the rock and, like an Indian hunter, peered through the fringe of bushes that crowned the highest point of the ridge. I could see the whole of the ledge now with the trampled grass and wild flowers. It was empty. Below and beyond it I could see neither the steep slope of the ridge nor could I see through the thick canopy of foliage below. I waited for perhaps ten minutes, fearful of emerging too soon from my hiding-place and finding either of them. Then cautiously I climbed down to the ledge, across the trampled greenery and as I reached the lip of the ledge I saw Wayne.

He was lying far below, head downward, his arms flung out, his face covered with blood.

Quickly I scrambled down to him. I bent over him and called his name again and again, but there was no answer at all. He was alive for he was breathing heavily. His shirt had been nearly torn from his back and left the whole upper part of his body exposed. In my frantic efforts to rouse him I remember one thing—the fleshliness and the beauty of the wounded body which I knew now was an instrument of evil, not because he had been guilty of an act of which most men are guilty, but because of the evil which was involved. I remember how fair his skin was and that I noticed what I had never noticed before—that where the heavy veins course through the heavy muscles of the shoulder they showed blue through the almost transparent skin like the veins in marble. My reactions were tormented and confused by what had gone before and by the very bewilderment of adolescence. I had the feeling of being overpowered by emotions which I could not possibly understand.

When I could not rouse him I ran to the stream below and because there was at hand nothing in which I could carry water and because he was a big and powerful man whom I could not possibly drag to the edge of the creek, I tore off my shirt and held it under the water. Then I returned and wrung the water from it into his face. Three times I repeated the action without result and then I thought, "I must go back to the farm and get help!"

I knew that I could not go to Henry's farm because I could not have faced either Vinnie or

Henry, nor could I fetch any neighbor. In my confusion, my instinct told me that this was a disaster which only my grandfather could perhaps know how to manage.

So I left him there, lying as he had fallen, and ran along the deer path toward the county road. A hundred yards from the county road in the thickest part of the path, I heard a horse neigh and remembered suddenly that Wayne had said he was taking out the new mare for exercise. The horse neighed again and following the sound, I found the mare tied to a sapling twenty or thirty yards from the path. Leading her out through the deer path to the road I swung myself up and set off at a gallop for Clarendon.

I was worried about Old Prince who I knew would try to follow me wherever I went. I turned back twice to see him lumbering along as rapidly as he was able and then in a turn of the road I lost him.

My grandfather must have seen me galloping wildly across the Valley and the bridge below the house for he was waiting for me at the horse block with Aunt Susan coming down the path from the verandah. Before I reined in the mare, he called out, "What is it? What's the matter?" And recognizing the mare, "Where's Wayne?"

I told him between gasps of breath, holding my side, how I had found Wayne and tried to revive him. I said that he must have fallen from the ledge. I did not yet want to tell my grandfather anything more. For the moment that was enough.

"Get Jasper and Red and the buckboard," said my grandfather. "And tell the boys to harness Old Ben for Aunt Susan to drive to Masonville for the doctor. And see that they walk the mare until she cools off."

He went quickly into the house and I went to the stable. Before I had given all the orders, the news spread to the cabins and the women and children began to gather muttering and whispering. One of the women began to cry.

While Red superintended the harnessing of the horses he kept asking me the details of what had happened. There was a curious look in his eye. I told him the same story I had told my grandfather and said, "That's all I know." He looked at me as if he knew I was lying and said, "That's a hell of a place for him to go alone!" But I did not know then that the suspicions he had concerned me directly.

Then in the hubbub everyone seemed to forget me. The conveyances came around to the door. Aunt Susan drove off for Masonville this time willing that Old Ben should be as skittish as he pleased and then my grandfather left with Red and Jasper. In the back of the buckboard they placed one of the stretchers they always took to the Circuit Races in case of accidents. My grandfather said, "Maybe you'd better go along, Ronnie, to show the way." But Red said unexpectedly, "Judge I know the spot, exactly!"

I said, "There's a deer trail off the county road that leads you."

"I know! I know!" Red repeated with a sullen air. "It brings you right to the ridge."

Then they drove off and it struck me as odd that Red should know where the ledge was. I remembered that both times I had been to the ledge, the grass had been beaten down and I remembered again the woman's handkerchief. And then for the first time in my life it occurred to me how wrong were the people who thought that country life was a simple affair, in which nothing ever happened and that it was only city folk who knew excitement and romance and immorality. At school the boys, especially those who told the dirty stories, always treated me as if anyone who lived in the country was a yokel who could never know about such things.

Left alone in the Big House, I went to my room and lay on the bed, suddenly dead tired to the point of sickness. Lying there I tried to bring some order to my thoughts and decide what it was I should do. For the first time in my life I was forced to make a decision which affected deeply and perhaps tragically the lives of others and I was

214

without experience. What I knew was a heavy burden in itself for not only was the knowledge in itself a terrible thing, but by some strange chance I had been given a glimpse of what, even then I realized dimly, was a drama which contained the elements of temptation, of passion, of tragedy, and of evil.

The shock of the discovery of Vinnie's guilt left a kind of numbness in my spirit and somehow, perhaps rightly, the knowledge did not affect my deep feeling for her. I think I was aware then that I had played a small, unsought and unwanted role in a drama which touched the very depths of something which could be stronger than any of us. And I knew that Vinnie had struggled, but that the thing was stronger than herself or any power within her. I thought, "If love is like this it can be a frightening thing like . . . like death." For I could hear her voice, at first the strange voice of one who was hypnotized or enchanted, a voice which was Vinnie's but a voice which I did not know. And over against it, the caressing, sensual, desperate voice of Wayne—again a voice which was not Wayne's but of someone driven and reckless. I think the fact that I had not even seen them but only heard the quality of their voices made the experience the more frightening and impressive.

And after a long time I made that first decision of my life in which the lives of other people could be affected deeply. I decided that I would pretend that it had all happened exactly as I had described it. I would say that I had come upon Wayne by accident, finding him bleeding and unconscious. I would even improve the story by saying that Prince's barking had led me to him. Wayne might die. He might even be dead by now. If he were dead, Vinnie would be free of him and no one would ever know what happened but herself and me, and she did not even know that I shared her knowledge and in a strange way her sense of guilt. And then suddenly I heard again in my imagination the voice of Wayne—that strange, soft, sensual voice of whose evil I had had intimations since the summer before without understanding them. I heard that voice saying what I myself was thinking at that very moment. "What people don't know can't hurt them." I wondered briefly whether this was an immoral and corrupting philosophy and quickly dismissed the consideration, for my instinct told me that there was one person I loved who must not be hurt no matter what happened and that was Henry. For the first time I think I understood the full quality of his goodness and his innocence, and somehow I knew that this lay at the root of the terrible anguish in Vinnie's voice. Although Wayne had used the argument for his own passionate ends, it had value now in another way. I understood for the first time that sometimes there were great virtues in compromise. Henry must not be hurt.

There was only one thing which troubled me and that was why Vinnie had gone through all that when she could have saved herself by staying away.

But Wayne was not dead. It was nearly sundown when they returned driving slowly with Wayne on the stretcher in the back of the buckboard. He was not dead but he was still unconscious. They carried him up the path and into the house and up the winding stairs, and I kept watching and listening, hoping, half-praying that he would die since it would make Vinnie free and because if he died I should never have to face him again, with my gaze slipping away from him because I knew so much.

Aunt Susan and the doctor arrived a little while later and went upstairs. Supper was forgotten and when the doctor drove off my grandfather came into my room and stood beside the bed.

"He's very badly hurt," he said. "He has a fractured skull. The doctor can't say how it will turn out."

I didn't answer him and presently he said, "Ronnie, tell me again what happened . . . *exactly* as it happened!"

I repeated the story exactly as I had told it, adding only the detail regarding Prince's barking. Fortunately it was nearly dark in the room for if there had been light, he would have seen that I did not look at him and have known that I was lying. Even so, I think he suspected me, for he said, "Are you sure that's *exactly* what happened?"

I said, "Yes, Grandad." And then I asked if they had found Prince on the way to the Wild Country for I could not get out of my mind the picture of the poor old dog, trying so hard to keep up with the galloping horse.

He said, "No." And quickly I said, "I want to go back and look for him."

He said, "You needn't do that. The old dog will find his way back. He knows the country."

"Please let me go, Grandad." But he said, "If he doesn't come back by the time we've finished supper, we'll take a lantern and go and look for him."

"I don't think I want any supper."

I shouldn't have said that for again it made him suspicious. He said, "Come now! You can't be that upset by what happened. You're a growing boy. You must at least have a glass of milk."

I wanted to say that I could have that in my room but I did not dare say it. I had to go down and sit at the table with him and Aunt Susan and the consciousness of my lie, acting as if nothing more than the accident had happened. I was learn-

ing fast the things one had to do in life as one
ceased to be a child.

Dinner was a gloomy affair with my Aunt Susan
leaving the table three or four times to go to the
sick room overhead until Jasper returned from
Masonville with the nurse. My grandfather was
troubled and I think still certain that he had not
heard all of the story. And I was worried now
mostly about old Prince. I kept seeing him, lost
and worn-out and alone somewhere in a fence corner and suddenly I decided that whether my
grandfather approved or not, I would steal out
of the house and go to search for him.

And then as Jackson brought the dessert, he
brought Prince with him. The old dog was covered with dust and mud and badly tired with his
tongue hanging out of one side of his mouth. At
sight of me, he came over, wagging his tail feebly
and put his head on my knee. I leaned down and
put my face against his. He licked my ear and then
flung himself down beside me.

The nurse arrived a little later, a pretty dark-
haired woman of perhaps twenty-six or -seven
years old called Mrs. Hallam. Aunt Susan put
her in the room next to Wayne. My grandfather went upstairs to sit for a time in Wayne's
room and I took Prince to the kitchen and gave
him a great bowl of food, but he only sniffed at
it, tried a mouthful or two and then refused to eat.

219

I poured milk for him but he would not drink it and only looked at me as if he were trying to explain that he was tired and ill. So I led him up to bed.

Usually he slept on a rug next to the bed where I could reach down in the night if I wakened and feel his rough coat there beside me. Always he would waken and lick my hand. But tonight I did what Aunt Susan had forbidden me to do. I took him on the great double bed. He tried feebly to climb up but could not make it and in the end I lifted him up and placed him on it. After I was in bed with the lights out I reached over and took one of his paws in my hand. Confused and tired and lonely as I was, the touch of the calloused paw was a singular comfort. In spite of everything I fell asleep quickly.

Just at daylight I wakened and reaching over found that the old dog was no longer there and sitting up in bed I looked about the room and then I found him close to the bed on his old rug, partly under the bed and I knew at once that something was wrong by the unnatural, stiff position of the legs. I got down and bent over him and then I discovered that he was dead. He must have gotten down from the bed during the night to die on the old rug.

I lifted his head and held it for a moment between my hands, looking at him, my eyes smarting with tears. He had been my friend as far back as I could remember since Henry's father had brought him over as a fat, wobbly puppy when my parents were drowned and I was not yet two years old.

There was nothing I could do so I climbed back into the bed and did a very childish thing. I pulled the bedclothes over my head and cried. I think the weeping did good for the tension went out of me slowly, but even in the midst of my tears, I kept thinking that it was Wayne who had killed him. His death was a part of all the driving evil of what Wayne had done and beyond that of the forces which had driven him.

I do not believe that my Aunt Susan had any suspicions that I had lied or at least held back part of the truth but like many people with a strong love for birds and animals, she had fantastic powers of intuition and she knew that something was wrong, something more than the death of old Prince.

She said, "I'll ask Jasper to dig a grave up in the burial ground and we can bury him this evening. But I think you'd better drive over with me to Henry's this afternoon and see the baby. After all he's your godson and he's named for you and they'll think it queer that you didn't come over at once to see him."

I told her that I had meant to do so the day

before and would have stopped there but for the accident to Wayne. I knew that there was no escaping the visit. I wanted to see them and the baby but at the same time I dreaded the meeting with Vinnie. But before we started Henry himself drove up. The news of Wayne's "accident" had spread through all the Valley, and he had come over as soon as he heard it to ask how Wayne was and whether he could be of any help.

He put his arm about my shoulders while he talked to Aunt Susan and then he turned to me and said, "My governor! How you've grown! In another year you'll be taller than me." He laughed and said, "We're gettin' old, Ronnie. Now there's another Ronnie. I can remember when you were just his age. When are you coming over to see him?"

I said that we were planning to drive over just as he came up. His face grew suddenly serious and he said to Aunt Susan. "I'm glad you're coming over. Vinnie hasn't been very well lately. She doesn't sleep and she's lost a lot of weight. I think maybe something's gone wrong inside when the baby was born. She won't see Doc Lee. She says there's nothing the matter and it wouldn't do any good."

"I think I can tell pretty well by looking at her," said Aunt Susan. "If it's really bad I'll take her up to St. Louis to a specialist. How's Mrs. Durham working out?"

Mrs. Durham was a kind of country midwife and nurse, no longer young, who was living with Henry and Vinnie to help out now that there was a baby. Both Henry and Vinnie preferred that to taking on a hired man because Vinnie liked working in the fields and the barns and in many ways was better and certainly much smarter than an oafish "hired man."

"She's fine!"

"Then she could manage with the baby if we went to St. Louis?"

"I guess so. He's been weaned for a month. We've got him on good Jersey milk. Had to take some of the cream out of it. It was too rich."

Then Aunt Susan said we'd better be going as she had to be back when the specialist returned from St. Louis.

I rode over with Henry because we had so much to talk about and Aunt Susan followed in the dog-cart. Henry was in high spirits save for his worry about Vinnie's "going off her feed" and he wanted to hear all about my trip to the Old Country.

He listened while I answered his questions in a different way from that in which he had listened to me in the past. It was as if he had become the boy and I had become the man. Presently he said, "I've always thought I'd like to make a trip like

223

that. I'd like to get around some, but I guess there ain't much chance what with the farm work and a family starting. Looks like I'd never get very far from the Valley."

The prospect did not appear to trouble him very greatly. So far as he knew, a good life lay before him, all ordered and complete and secure with a world of his own within his farm and the Valley. In many ways he was the most fortunate of men. Yet even with him the security of his world was, in one sense, only an illusion. Perhaps he knew about Vinnie's past; I never found out how much he knew or if he really knew anything at all. What he did not know was what had happened on the ledge and how near his secure little world really was to collapse and ruin. The odd thing was that the salvation of his world lay not in fact but in an illusion—in his never finding out what had happened. The preservation of that illusion so far as I knew then, lay in the hands of three people—Vinnie, myself and Wayne who might die as at that moment I hoped earnestly he would.

Vinnie was nowhere to be seen when we arrived and Henry said, "Go right on in. I expect she's feeding the baby. I'll take care of the horses and be right in."

So Aunt Susan, who had followed us in the dogcart, and I opened the gate and walked to the back porch where Aunt Susan opened the screen door and led the way in, calling out "Vinnie! Vinnie!"

There was no answer at first and then Mrs. Durham, a kindly, gossipy old woman who looked rather like a gnarled oak, came out of the hallway.

She said, "Good morning, Miss Susan— Good morning, Ronnie. Mrs. Vinnie is in the bedroom. She says to come on in."

She had been changing the baby's diapers and he sat now in her lap, dark-haired and dark-eyed like Henry. She smiled at us but there was no life in the smile. Her tanned skin looked sallow and there were deep circles under her eyes. It was a smile of affection she gave us but the old quiet happy radiance wasn't in it.

"Well, Ronnie!" she said, "It's good to see you. Come over here and look at the new little Ronnie."

I moved to her trying my best to act as if I knew nothing, as if nothing at all had happened. And I kept thinking how kind she had been to me the last time I had seen her on the night I went away. Then she looked down at the baby and an extraordinary light came into her eyes that wiped out all else. It was the look of a woman who was meant to have many children.

The baby was a beauty. He didn't have that ungainly awkward look that many boy babies have. He was neat and compact and complete like Henry, already a little man. I thought, "When he's bigger I can take him out and show him the Valley as Henry showed it to me."

Then Vinnie invited us to have some fresh-made cider and we went out on the porch and in the full light the effects of suffering in her face were even clearer. Mrs. Durham brought the cider and some glasses and poured it and Vinnie held the baby on her knees, bouncing him a little. He was a healthy child and liked the bouncing and as I watched it struck me that Vinnie, whom I had always thought of as passably good-looking and changeable, was really very beautiful.

The women gossiped but I didn't hear much of what they said for I was all churned up inside, but one thought came to me which returned many times in after life—that Vinnie inside herself, must be two people and that maybe all interesting people were like that, not simple and complete and compact like Henry, but complex and change-able and many people in one body. I loved Henry and he had shown and taught me many fascinating things, but in himself he was not really interesting but only kind and good and wholesome and inno-cent. And I kept thinking how different was this maternal Vinnie, with her hair wound in braids about her head, from the Vinnie whose voice had cried out, "Why don't you leave me alone? If you don't leave me alone, I'll get a gun and kill you!"

On the way home Aunt Susan said, "Henry's right. She looks very ill. I'll have to persuade her to go up to St. Louis with me and see a specialist." And of course I could have told Aunt Susan what the illness was and that the trip would be unnecessary but I could not.

We were late for lunch and my grandfather and the brain specialist were eating. He was a plump, pink-faced, bald little man with very bright eyes. He explained to us what he had already told my grandfather—that Wayne had a fractured skull and a serious concussion and that it might be days before he recovered consciousness. There would be no use in moving him all the way to St. Louis; it might even do him harm. He had left medicines with the nurse. If there were no blood clots or complications he would be all right although it might take weeks for him to recover. The doctor went off to Masonville to the train driven by Jasper, and my grandfather went up to Wayne's room.

That evening Jasper and I carried old Prince, wrapped in a good white cotton sheet contributed by Aunt Susan, up to the graveyard next to the orchard where the other dogs and the famous Clarendon stallions and mares were buried, each with its own small headstone. The graveyard covered an area of about two acres, largely overgrown with periwinkle and surrounded by a white picket fence. Aunt Susan followed us and stood with me while Jasper placed the old dog gently on the fresh yellow clay. The smarting tears came into my eyes again and then Aunt Susan and I walked back in silence through the orchard to the Big House. I dreaded going to bed for it would be the first time in my life that I had gone to bed at Clarendon without Prince at my side where I could reach out and touch his rough coat when I wakened in the still night.

Then for ten days little happened at all. I went over two or three times to see Vinnie, Henry and the baby, and Aunt Susan failed to persuade Vinnie to go to St. Louis to the doctor. This was remarkable for Aunt Susan, although a small woman, had the power of a dynamo combined with that of a steam roller and nearly always had her way in the end. Vinnie was the only person I have ever known who was wholly successful against her persistence and bullying but Vinnie revealed an extraordinary streak of peasant stubbornness. She said, "There is nothing the matter with me. I'm strong as an ox. Why should I go to St. Louis and waste Henry's good money?"

And then I was sure that Vinnie would look no better until Wayne either died or left the Valley forever and I began trying to think of some way by which I could, without betraying anything, induce my grandfather once Wayne recovered, never to let him return.

But it wasn't only Vinnie who looked "peaked." One day my grandfather said sharply to me, "What's the matter with you, Ronnie? I speak to you and you don't hear me. I ask you questions and I have to repeat them two or three times. Is there anything the matter?"

I told him that there was nothing the matter—that I was just thinking.

"Haven't you ever thought before?"

"Yes. Why, yes, of course!"

But even when I said that I was lying because I had only begun to *think* quite lately. I believe the process began on the day I had lunch with my grandmother in Salzburg. Until then I had lived largely by emotions and senses, daydreaming, yes, but not thinking. With the shock of the happening on the limestone ridge in the Wild Country, the process had increased enormously. I seemed to be *thinking* all the time until sometimes my head hurt —about what had happened there, about what people were like on the inside, even people like Jasper who seemed outwardly as simple as a little child, about the curious physical attraction and the spiritual repulsion which Wayne created in me, about the way my love for Henry had been transferred or shared with Vinnie as the object, about what it was that had kept my grandmother and Chastel together for so long in the face of many obstacles so that she cared for him like a child now that he was old and ill and blind. There was so much to think about that there seemed never to be enough time, and being innocent there were many things that bewildered me. Yes, in those days I kept thinking until my head hurt.

Aunt Susan said, "It may be that you're bilious. Stick out your tongue." She regarded it for a second and said, "My goodness, yes! You'd better take two liver pills when you go to bed," and bustled off to fetch them.

But it wasn't my liver which was out of order. Something much more profound was the matter with me, and I believe my grandfather was by now convinced of it as well as of the fact that it had something to do with Wayne and his accident. He had not long to wait in order to find out.

Then one morning Wayne was conscious for a little while and the nurse fetched my grandfather to the room but he got nothing out of Wayne for when he returned downstairs where Aunt Susan and I were waiting, he said, "He had a little difficulty talking but he says he doesn't remember anything at all except falling. Then he faded out again." He frowned and said, "I guess we'll have to wait till he's better to find out the whole story —if we ever find it out. It's so unlikely that a big, strong fellow like Wayne could just *fall*. In fact it's damned unlikely that he'd be spending his time wandering about that swamp or climbing ridges. He never gave a damn about nature except to go shooting and there isn't anything to shoot at this time of year and anyway he wasn't even carrying a gun."

Red returned again from the Circuit for a week end and late on Sunday afternoon just as he left for Masonville to take the train, my grandfather came up to my room where I was reading. He came in and closed the door behind him and I knew at once that he had learned something.

He said "Hello!" casually, and then said, "There's something I want to talk about, Ronnie."

I said, "Yes, Grandad," and put down my book.

Then he said, as he had done so often, "Let's pretend we're a couple of men talking things over."

My heart began to beat wildly. I wasn't afraid. I was confused as if all the thoughts, the deep troubling, complex thoughts, were churning round in my head. I didn't say anything but I felt myself blushing and he said, "Red just told me something. He said that Old Virgil is telling the story that Wayne wasn't alone in the swamp. He says that he was coming along the country road just after noon on the day Wayne was hurt and that he saw Vinnie coming out of the swamp where the deer path crosses the road. He says her hair was all loose and that her dress was torn and that she was crying. He says that when she saw him, she ran back again into the bushes and hid. Red says Old Virgil told the Kleinfelter girl and that she's giggling and telling the story too." He looked at me directly. "You understand that we've got to stop Old Virgil from telling that story. I think I could shut him up if it's necessary. I think I might be able even to send him to jail. I don't want to and I can't stop him unless I know what I'm talking about. It's got to be done for Vinnie's sake and for Henry's. I know you want to help them."

"Yes."

"Maybe you can help more than anyone if you work with me. I know there's something you haven't told me. Did you *know* that Wayne wasn't alone?"

It was coming now! I braced myself and tried to imagine that I was a man talking to another man and that I knew the answers to all the things that had troubled me, but it was no good. I just didn't know, and I knew it!

I said, "Yes."

"Was it Vinnie who was with him?"

"Yes."

The answer seemed to shock him as much as my discovery of Wayne and Vinnie had shocked me. For a second he could not speak. Then he said, "Did you see them?"

"No."

"No?" He was puzzled and then asked, "Then how did you know they were together?"

"I heard them."

Again he was puzzled and then he said, "Don't make me drag it out of you, Ronnie. You tell it your own way. You understand we've got to straighten this thing out."

So, painfully at first and then gradually more easily, I told him how I had gone away early to escape Wayne and had gone to the peak of the ridge to eat my lunch and had fallen asleep and wakened to hear their voices.

Here he interrupted me and said, "What was it they said? Can you tell me, Ronnie?"

I told him as well as I could remember what they had said and about Vinnie's resistance and her sobbing and all the other details and he asked me, "Did you understand what was happening?"

"Yes, Grandad, I did. But I couldn't go away. I didn't dare move. I was afraid they'd discover me."

"Yes, that was right. There wasn't anything else you could do."

He was silent for a moment and then he asked, "She was fighting him?"

"Yes . . . I think she was fighting herself too." And then quickly I said, "I didn't tell you. I didn't tell anyone because I thought only Vinnie and I and Wayne knew about it. They didn't know I was there and I thought Wayne wouldn't tell or that he might die and then nobody would know but Vinnie and myself."

He looked at me with a faint smile. "You were quite right, Ronnie. It was a very wise thing you did. It would have been all right if Old Virgil hadn't come along. I had to know, you see, whether he was just lying. It may be that you'll have to help me some more. Can I count on you?"

"Yes, Grandad."

"And you mustn't think too ill of Vinnie. There are other things I have to find out before we can judge."

"I don't think ill of Vinnie," I said. "I love her. I know she didn't want it to happen."

Again he was thoughtful and I knew that we were thinking the same thing. Why had she gone there in the first place?

After a moment he asked, "Why did you hit Wayne on the day you came home and say 'don't do that' when he rumpled your hair?"

"I don't know. It just happened without thinking. I couldn't help doing it."

As he talked his face seemed slowly to lose its color and he looked suddenly very old. He asked, "Did Wayne ever talk to you about things like this? Did he ever talk. . . ." He seemed to be reaching for a word or a phrase and finally he said, "Did he ever talk in an evil way when he was alone with you?"

"No. It wasn't anything he said."

"What was it then? I noticed that there was something wrong between you."

"I don't know. It wasn't anything he said. It was something I felt. I guess that sounds pretty silly but it's true. Once when we were in the stable with Red they got to talking about women. I guess some of the talk was pretty dirty. I didn't understand some of it."

"He shouldn't have done that."

He said this with a curious sadness and it dawned on me that something terrible was happening inside him, that in some ways at least he knew less of Wayne than either Vinnie or I knew, that the Wayne who had existed up to now in his mind had been the bright, good-looking, healthy country boy he had helped through college, of whose success he had always been so proud. I do not know how much he knew or suspected of the curious corruption which I, so much younger and so much less experienced, had felt instinctively with the sensitivity of the adolescent. If he had had any doubts or suspicions I think he deliberately put them out of his mind, for in a way Wayne had long ago taken the place in his heart of my dead father.

He was asking me, "Do you think that the fall was an accident?"

"I don't know. I didn't see anything. It sounded as if he was struggling with her and as if one of

235

them had struck the other. Then I heard her scream and I waited for a long time and when I didn't hear anything I climbed down and found him lying there."

He rose and came over, put his hand on my head and said, "Thank you, Ronnie. I think you were right to hold back the truth. If Old Virgil hadn't happened onto it, everything might have been all right. The old fool seems always to be making trouble. I think I'll have to talk to Vinnie and maybe you'd better come along with me."

Desperately I said, "No, Grandad. It would be better without me."

"I'll have to think it all over. We can decide in the morning." His hand slipped down to my shoulder, "I'm sorry it had to happen to you. It's tough on you. But don't fuss about it. We'll work it out."

Before he turned to go I said, "There's one thing, Grandad. If Wayne gets well he oughtn't ever come back to the Valley."

He looked at me sharply as if I had given him casually the one bit of information he wanted above all else. "Do you mean he has done evil here?"

"Yes . . . I suppose that's it."

Then he said, "I'd thought of that already." And then he left me but in the doorway he turned and said, "Remember this is between the two of us. It doesn't even include your Aunt Susan." But as we found out later Aunt Susan in some ways already knew more of Vinnie's story than we knew.

In the morning my grandfather said, "Wayne is much better this morning. He still says he remembers nothing, and I suppose he will always say that. I'm going over to talk to Vinnie. I want you to go with me. Maybe I'll need you, maybe I won't, but don't fuss about it. By some good luck Henry has gone to Masonville for the day."

Again I protested and even struggled against going with him but he said, "I know you want to help Vinnie and Henry. If I don't need you, I won't drag you into it. I promise you that!"

I don't know how he discovered that Henry was absent but it *was* a great stroke of luck, one of those small things which happen when it seems that some cycle of chance or perhaps even of design intervenes in human affairs.

When we arrived at Henry's place, my grandfather said, "You go out to the barn and amuse yourself there. Keep out of sight and if I want you I'll call you."

I obeyed him and he never called me until everything was over and Vinnie had disappeared again into the house, so on that morning I never saw her at all.

My grandfather went into the house and found Vinnie doing the washing and he said, "Vinnie. Could we have a talk?"

The color went out of her face and for a moment he thought she was going to faint and then she caught herself, holding on to the edge of the washtub and said, "Yes, Judge!"

He proposed that they go to the orchard which lay behind the old house and she followed him walking, he said, as if she were hypnotized. They sat on a bench which Henry had put up at the far end of the orchard where there was a beautiful view of the Wild Country and my grandfather said, "First of all, Vinnie, I'm on your side and I'm going to stick by you. You know that all of us are your friends?"

Still as if in a trance, she answered, "Yes, Judge!"

Then he asked, "Is it true that Old Virgil saw you coming out of the swamp the day Wayne had his accident?"

"Yes, Judge!"

"That's good. I wanted to know that. There's another thing you don't know." She looked up at him without speaking and he said, "Ronnie knew you were there too!"

This revelation seemed to terrify her and the tears came into her eyes and she cried out, "No! No! That can't be it! That can't be!"

"He was there all the time," said my grandfather. "He was above you on the peak above the ledge. He never saw you but he heard everything and when at last he came out he found Wayne. You must understand that he didn't mean to listen. He couldn't help himself. He never told me until I heard what Old Virgil was saying and I forced him to. Now what we have to do is straighten this thing out and I want to help. You can't do it alone. You must remember that I'm a lawyer and a judge and I understand many things you couldn't possibly understand. And I have a lot of power in the Valley. But most of all, we want to keep it away from Henry. Does he know anything?"

Quietly she answered, "No, I'm sure of that!"

"There's one thing you can do to help. You can tell me everything about the story. Will you do that?"

She looked down at her work-worn hands and said, "I don't know. I don't know if I can." But almost at once she began to tell him, pouring the story out passionately.

She began by telling him what she had already told Aunt Susan, of her seduction by Wayne while she was working at the boardinghouse, of the baby and what happened to her afterward and the details of her marriage to Henry. She never once looked at him but simply stared down at her

239

hands. My grandfather was suffering too, not only for her but because he was hearing, bit by bit, the story of Wayne's evil. Word by word she was destroying the man he had befriended, helped, and looked upon as a son.

She said, "When I came here, I never knew that Wayne would ever come here too. I thought I had cut off the past and that everything would be all right, but then one day Henry said that Wayne Torrance was coming to visit the Big House and I was frightened. I couldn't let anyone find out I'd known him and I made up my mind to keep out of sight till he had gone away again. But it turned all my happiness to misery. I thought of going away to visit my family or of going away altogether but I couldn't because I knew I was going to have the baby. It was Henry's baby too and he was excited about it. Sometimes in the evening he'd talk of nothing else but how wonderful it was going to be as we grew older and had a family.

"I couldn't go away and I couldn't stay. And the morning Miss Susan came to help me with the pickles, he turned up here with Ronnie and Miss Susan, and Miss Susan and Henry both wanted me to meet him. I couldn't hide. I couldn't do anything because I was scared of making people wonder what was the matter. So I came out and met him acting like I'd never seen him before.

Anyway I tried but I thought I was going to die. And he acted the same way and it was all right for then. Nobody seemed to guess anything. But all day I thought I was going to die. I had to go and lay down and then I felt I had to tell somebody.

"I guess it was because Miss Susan had been so good to me when everybody else in the Valley treated me like a chippy. And I knew too that Miss Susan was helping me that day because she wanted me to win at the County Fair. I knew and she knew, I guess, that that would help me more than anything else. I couldn't bear it any more and so I told Miss Susan everything that had happened before I came here, only I didn't tell her who the man was.

"And then he went away the next day and I felt better. I kept hoping and telling myself that maybe he wouldn't come back or that maybe he'd be killed or die and then everything would be all right because there wasn't anybody else in the world who would remember me, and then Henry and I and everything we had here would be safe."

Then she was silent for a moment, wringing her hands as if in anguish, and the tears came into her eyes and she said, as if she were being tortured, "You see, Judge, I was afraid of myself too."

When the baby came and it was a boy which pleased Henry and satisfied her peasant heart, she almost forgot about Wayne. The fear of him would return sometimes in the night, sometimes when she was working alone in the house. And it wasn't only the fear of Wayne but of herself if she ever found herself alone with him. And then one day she had a letter from Wayne, saying that he was coming on a long visit and that he wanted to see her alone and talk to her. It was at the same time a passionate love letter. She could not even bring herself to tell my grandfather what was in it, but it was clear that he had written with the cold and calculated intent of rousing in her the thing she had fought so valiantly to suppress. At the end he had written, "Of course, nobody ever need know about it if you meet me. There are plenty of places in the Valley. It's perfectly safe. Think what it would be like again!"

I think his interest was no greater than simply the desire to provide himself with a woman during the three weeks' visit. The life at Clarendon bored him after a day or two and with his great vigor and sensuality he could not go for long without a woman.

Because of my grandfather he could not go wolfing about openly in the Valley and he could do nothing in Masonville which would not be discovered. The situation with Vinnie was set up naturally for him, especially as he knew, I think, that once he could induce her to meet him he could do with her as he pleased. The curious thing was, I think, that in his amorality he saw nothing evil in what he was doing. He really believed that he could resume his relationship with Vinnie without hurting anyone so long as they never found out. I think too that while he had no real feeling for nature and the woods and fields, the prospect of carrying on a love affair hidden away in such surroundings excited him.

The letter terrified her.

She said, "I burned it quickly in the stove but now I was afraid again—more afraid than ever for fear some morning Henry would go for the mail instead of me and find a letter from him and ask me about it. You see, Judge, nobody ever wrote to me except sometimes about twice a year, my mother."

"But he didn't write again. I didn't even know when he was coming. I thought again of going away but I would have to take the baby and there was no place to go. I knew if I said I was going and asked Henry for some money, he'd give it to me and when I got to thinking about that it made everything worse. And then we'd got Mrs. Durham here to work in the house so I could help Henry with the cows and he could work longer in the fields and if I went away everything would be upset." Again she began to cry and said, "And

243

all the time I *wanted* to see him again. That was the worst of all!"

And then one evening while Henry was working late on the far end of the farm Vinnie went down to the lower pasture to fetch the cows and saw coming toward her the figure of a man on a horse and almost at once she knew who it was. She tried to hide in the willows along the creek, but he had seen her and rode directly to where she was hiding. He tried to seduce her all over again then and there but she was afraid because Mrs. Durham and Henry had known that she had gone to fetch the cows and might have seen Wayne riding across the field.

On that occasion when she left him he said, "It's better that we meet again without anyone finding out than if we don't meet and people do find out."

She understood what he meant and in fear of his blackmail, she agreed to meet him because the thing had to be settled once and for all and inside her there was a strange tumult because the sight of him had aroused in her all the old memories and desires.

In her clumsy English and with a bitter anguish, she tried to explain to my grandfather. She said, "You see, Judge, I love Henry. I love my baby. I love my life here. I love this orchard and the house and the barns and the cattle. I love them better than being alive. But this other thing was

244

different. It was like I was two women. If Wayne had married me maybe everything would have been all right because I did love him so much I was afraid of him but it was different—like I was two different women.

"So I told him I'd meet him and he said did I know that place in the swamp and I said I did because when I first came here Henry took me there to show me how beautiful the swamp was and then afterward sometimes when I had a couple of hours to myself, I'd go there alone. You see when I was frightened or worried I'd go there alone and afterward I always felt better because I guess I didn't seem so important or what happened to me so important. And three days later after Henry had gone to the fields, I left the baby with Mrs. Durham and went there. I was afraid and I even thought of taking Henry's gun along and shooting him if he wouldn't leave me alone. But I didn't. I guess I had sense enough to know that it could only make matters worse."

So she went to the ridge and she tried to explain to Wayne how she had a good life and a good husband she loved and he must let her alone, but he wasn't interested in that. He only wanted one thing and he wouldn't even listen but began making love to her passionately, and then it was that I wakened and heard the voices and the sobbing and the final scream.

She said, "He didn't fall. I pushed him! I don't know whether I meant to push him or not but when he began wanting me to do it all over again I went kind of crazy and attacked him. I hit him and hit him in the face and then he fell over the edge and I went away. I didn't even stop to see if he was hurt. I wanted him to die." She looked up from her hands and out across the Wild Country. "And then as I came running out of the swamp there was Old Virgil driving along the road. I tried to hide quick but he must have seen me. That's all there is, Judge. There is only one thing I care about on earth. I don't want Henry to be hurt and I don't want anything to happen to this place. If that happened I could take a gun and go and find Wayne and kill him no matter where he was, and then maybe I'd kill myself."

They sat in silence for a time and then my grandfather said, "You go back to the house, Vinnie, and try to act as if nothing is the matter. I promise you two things . . . I'll see to it that Wayne never comes back to the Valley and that he never bothers you again. And I'll shut up Old Virgil. The talk hasn't gone very far, and Henry is likely to be the last man in the Valley to hear it. I think maybe I can force Old Virgil to say he just made the story up. It's going to be all right."

Then suddenly she began to cry and could not stop for a long time and when at last she was quieted my grandfather said, "Go and take a walk down across the pasture and back again and bathe your eyes in the creek before you go back to the house. Mrs. Durham is a good old soul but she's awfully curious and gossipy. She might ask you questions. And when you come back act as if nothing has happened."

Then he left her and went to fetch me at the barn where I had been kicking my heels and waiting impatiently for more than two hours. As we harnessed the horse the figure of Henry, riding seated on the broad back of one of the Percheron team, appeared at the far end of the lane. I said, "Look, there's Henry!" But my grandfather said, "We didn't see him" and quickly turned Old Ben down the lane to the road.

He was silent for a long time and presently he said, "It was exactly as you said. I think it was a good thing we drove over to talk to Vinnie."

And then as we drove along the Valley road he told me, bit by bit, slowly as if it hurt him, what had happened between them. He told it as if Wayne were a stranger, and I think that Wayne had become so. He did say, "This is a tangled business, son, and you mustn't make flash judgments about anybody. Vinnie is a good woman and she's suffered terribly. She never had a chance and we've got to help her now. And Wayne . . . well, he's just a biological phenomenon. Nature

247

made him that way. He's healthy and strong and She meant him to breed and breed and She gives him no peace. I'm not excusing him. I'm afraid it is stronger in him than anything I've been able to do for him." Then he was silent for a moment and said, "Maybe that's what you felt in him. Maybe that's what changed everything between you." He looked at me suddenly and said, "Were you afraid of him?" And after a moment I said, "Yes. I guess that was it."

Then a faint smile came into his thin face, "Your Aunt Susan is very sly—never telling me anything about what Vinnie has told her." He sighed deeply and then said, "And now we've got to stop and shut Old Virgil's mouth. It's going to be hard."

But he didn't have to shut Old Virgil's mouth for fate had already done it. As we passed through the covered bridge and rounded the thick woods and came suddenly upon Virgil's run-down house, the Kleinfelter girl came running out to meet us. She was in a high state of excitement, her hair streaming behind her back from the silly round face. She ran up to us and said, "Come in the house, Judge! Virgil and the Missus are dead sick."

My grandfather pulled up the horse and asked, "What do you mean?"

"Virgil is frothin' at the mouth. He's all swole up and the Missus can't talk."

He handed the reins to me and went into the house while I tied Old Ben to the hitching rail. Then I followed him through the open door. I found him in Mattie's bedroom, that dreadful room with drawn shades, smelling of flannel and medicine and kerosene even in midsummer. He was bending over Virgil's wife who lay there like a withered mummy. The thin, querulous face had a grotesque appearance for the lips were horribly swollen so that she seemed to have grown a kind of snout. My grandfather had one arm behind her back and had lifted her up. As he did so, her head with the grey hair braided in two short, ratty pigtails fell forward on the chest covered by a grey nightgown made of outing flannel. The Kleinfelter girl was standing a little way off and there was a curious, bright glitter in her small eyes. My grandfather shook the old woman very gently as if to rouse her but the head only wobbled back and forth. Then he laid her back on the soiled pillow and said, "She's dead already!"

Quickly he turned to the Kleinfelter girl and said, "Where's Virgil?" And at the same time the sound of Virgil's groans came through the door. They began with a moaning sound and ended with an anguished cry which sounded like "Oh! Oh! Oh!"

The girl said, "He's in the sittin' room. I guess he's pretty bad off."

We found Old Virgil in the rocking chair, writhing and groaning and clutching his stomach. His lips, like those of the old woman, were grotesquely swollen and he was beyond speech. I think he recognized my grandfather. He managed to turn his head a little way and give one gleam filled with terror in our direction and then he fell forward in convulsions.

My grandfather said to me, "It acts like arsenic poisoning. Go and drive fast for Doc Lee." And then to the Kleinfelter girl, "Get me milk! Lots of it! Quick!"

I drove Old Ben as hard as he could stand it into Masonville and I had to wake Doc Lee who was having his after lunch nap. But it was no good. By the time we got back to the farm, Old Virgil was dead too.

There wasn't any doubt about it. Old Virgil and Mattie had been poisoned and with arsenic. But who had done it or where the arsenic had come from was the question. Of course the Kleinfelter girl was the obvious suspect and when the sheriff came he ordered her to pack up her belongings and go with him to town. That left Old Virgil and Mattie alone in the house with only the undertaker.

The house itself looked, as Aunt Susan said, like a poorly managed hog pen. Mattie's room was as it always had been. The rest of the house had not been cleaned for months and in the kitchen the soiled dishes were piled high. It seemed that Emma Kleinfelter's system had been to use all the pans and dishes in the house and then wash them all at once.

Late that afternoon, Aunt Susan drove around recruiting some stout neighbors to help her and the following morning they assembled and gave the place the first real cleaning it had had since Mattie took to her bed more than twenty years earlier. Everybody in the Valley went to funerals, and this was more certain than most funerals to attract everyone so Aunt Susan thought the least she and the neighbors could do was to have the house looking nice when they came to carry Virgil and Mattie to the burial ground at the Valley church. It took them the whole of the day to put the house in order. Mattie's bed clothes they simply carried out on the end of a broom and burned at the end of the weedy garden.

As for Emma Kleinfelter, the county sheriff, the coroner, and the prosecuting attorney in Masonville all questioned her, but what information they got from her led nowhere. She told them that the breakfast she made that morning for Virgil and Mattie had included fried eggs and fried potatoes, coffee and *Schmierkäse*. In the *Schmierkäse* lay the only clue, for Emma said she had eaten eggs and the fried potatoes and the coffee but not the *Schmierkäse*. Both Virgil and Mattie had eaten it. It was kept, she said, in the springhouse against the hill back of the house along with the cream and the butter. Someone, she thought, might have come in the night and put poison in it. This was Emma's own theory and it was not an illogical one for Virgil had quarrelled at some time or other with most of his neighbors and did not speak to most of them. My grandfather once said that he guessed the people at Clarendon were the only people in the township whom Virgil spoke to. While they questioned her the Kleinfelter girl sat hunched up in a corner of the jail office, watching them out of her small pig-faced eyes. She didn't seem afraid or show any sign of guilt and when at last they had wearied of asking her questions they took her away to the county home because she was only sixteen and under the law they couldn't properly lock her up in the county jail.

Aunt Susan came home worn out from the house-cleaning and said at supper that it looked as if the stars had conspired together to bring down tragedy and confusion upon the Valley that summer.

But the news of Wayne was good. The doctor from St. Louis had been there again in the afternoon and said that the clot was dissolving and that he'd probably be all right in another two or three weeks. He was quite conscious that day when he was awake but he still slept a great deal.

They buried Old Virgil and Mattie side by side in the Valley church burial ground so that even in death they were together although for more than twenty years they had hated each other with a snarling animal hatred. There was a great crowd at the funeral and people trampled through the house and went to the springhouse where the *Schmierkäse* had been kept. There were reporters down from St. Louis who wrote stories with headlines like "End of Sordid Country Tragedy. Mystery Still Unsolved."

The investigation, they wrote, was still in progress and suspicion now pointed to two possibilities—that Virgil and Mattie Plotz had been poisoned by a neighbor who had a feud with Virgil, or that Virgil himself had poisoned his wife and himself. Those of us who knew Virgil did not credit the second theory unless he had bungled in his attempt to kill Mattie alone and poisoned himself along with her by mistake. People who kill themselves have a capacity for suffering, and Virgil had little or none. We knew, too, that Virgil had nourished his hatred for Mattie for years and thrived upon it. It gave him in a way his only claim to notice for he never failed to talk of the misery it was for a man to have a wife who was "no good." It wasn't likely that Virgil would destroy his one claim to notice.

And then ten days later the papers announced that Emma Kleinfelter, the hired girl, had been released from custody and had returned to live with her father, a farmer, on the edge of the Wild Country.

During this time, my grandfather was away a great deal. Sometimes I went with him on his frequent visits to Masonville and to the crossroads settlements and eventually to every farm in the Valley, farms he had not visited in years or had never visited at all. It was as if he were running a political campaign and it was not till after I had taken several trips with him that I discovered what he was doing. Wherever he went, no matter whom he talked to, the murder of Virgil and Mattie came into the conversation sooner or later. Most people, knowing my grandfather was a judge and a lawyer, believed he would know more about such things than they and asked his opinion; but he never gave any. And then sooner or later they would ask about Wayne, and grandfather would sometimes lead them on very skillfully into revealing they had heard that Henry Benson's wife had been seen coming out of the swamp by Old Virgil on the afternoon of Wayne's accident.

When that happened my grandfather would go into action. He would say that the story was a malicious lie and that he had at least three good reasons for knowing so. First, he said that as soon as Wayne had regained consciousness he himself described the accident, saying that he had ridden on horseback as far as he could go into the swamp and then dismounted and climbed the ridge. While he was standing there near the edge the rock had crumbled and fallen away and that was all he could remember. It had been a stroke of good fortune that his grandson Ronnie had happened along a little while later to find him. And then, if I was present, he would turn to me for verification. Secondly, the story couldn't be true because on that afternoon Henry Benson's wife had gone to Masonville with his own sister Susan. And thirdly, old Virgil had confessed as he was dying that the whole story was a lie and that he had told it out of spite against Henry and his wife.

I wondered at these magnificent lies coming out of my grandfather until I understood that quietly he was killing the story spread by Old Virgil and the Kleinfelter girl and that he was doing an excellent job of it, not only because he presented his evidence in the style of a court-room lawyer but because he was a lawyer and a judge and as an experienced man, he was able to meet every argument or insinuation.

But the sensation of the murder had over-shadowed and very nearly wiped out the gossip about Virgil's seeing Vinnie come out of the swamp. My grandfather was very skillful in never bringing up the subject; he always led other people into mentioning it first.

Twice we stopped at Henry's farm and talked to Vinnie. The sullen air of fear was gone from her, the paleness went out of her face and once or twice she laughed. Each time she brought out the baby when she came to the gate. Once I heard my grandfather say aside to her, "It's going to be all right."

But it wasn't easy between Vinnie and me. We tried to look at each other squarely but at first we never quite succeeded in doing so. It was not, I know, that she distrusted me. It was simply that she felt the knowledge which we shared had somehow raised a barrier between us and that she was ashamed. There was nothing I could do and I knew that the strain would continue to exist between us until I went away to school, so I did not accept Henry's invitation to come over and spend a night or two with them before I left. I was too young then to know that as time went on and the tragedy slipped into the past both Vinnie and I would grow used to the knowledge and that presently instead of remaining a barrier it would become a bond between us so that in later life when our glance met there would be a twinkle in our eyes and a sudden flash of understanding not untouched with humor as if we were two children who could say, "We know something the rest of you don't know." For that is exactly what happened when the threat of Wayne was removed forever by my grandfather and Vinnie bore six children for Henry and her life became solid and settled and impregnable.

But for many years the sense of awkwardness and of guilt, which in some strange way I shared with her, came between us. Indeed the last shadow of it did not wholly disappear until at last I married and had children of my own and Vinnie was a plump, strong woman of middle-age with a large and handsome family.

A few days before I went back to school, there was some trouble about the nurse Mrs. Hallam who complained to my grandfather that Wayne had recovered his strength almost too rapidly and had been annoying her by his amorousness. My grandfather assured her that she might as well leave and that he would set things right before she left.

He went up to reproach Wayne for his behavior and he evidently found the occasion a likely opportunity to reveal to Wayne that he knew the whole story of Vinnie. It must have been a painful interview, for the old man had been forced to kill the last vestiges of his faith and his pride in the boy he had taken off a Missouri farm and educated and guided to success. I cannot believe that my grandfather, with his intelligence, instinct and experience, did not have some suspicion as to the kind of man Wayne really was, but I think that through weakness and pride and affection he had fought to put the knowledge aside and to pretend it was unfounded or did not exist. People, even strong and intelligent ones, will sometimes turn aside from honesty and deliberately deceive themselves, hoping willfully that they are wrong, when disillusion corrodes the image of their affections. In this case the disillusionment came so suddenly and so violently that my grandfather could no longer deceive himself.

I do not know what he said to Wayne, but the conversation must have been bitterly painful to him and at least awkward for Wayne, although nothing touched or depressed Wayne for very long. I think this was so because of his great animal vitality and because the one great impetus of his existence was the satisfaction of his sensuality. I came to understand what my grandfather meant when he said, "I'm afraid that it is stronger than anything I have been able to do for him." Certainly, as I was beginning to learn, it was stronger than any force on earth, stronger even than hunger.

After the interview, my grandfather came down-stairs and said to me, "I've had a talk with Wayne. He will never come back to the Valley. I am going over now to tell Vinnie so that now perhaps she can forget him and what happened."

I thought it odd that he had qualified what he had said by the word "perhaps" but he knew well enough that one does not forget those things and that although Vinnie would never see him again, that part of herself which frightened her, would remember even when she was an old woman what had happened and the violence of the passion between herself and Wayne which Henry, for all her love for him, had never roused. That is the strongest hold which the sensuous have upon others—that they are able to create a kind of evil, passionate glory of the flesh which those less sensuous would not know otherwise and which they can never forget once they have known it. It is a dubious but magnificent glory which the mild-mannered, the timid, the unrealized never attain. They know neither its delights nor its bit-terness but exist always in a kind of half-world of mild colors and gentle and safe monotony. Cer-tainly neither Wayne with his sensuality and his power of corruption, nor Vinnie with her close-ness to the earth and all living things, was among these.

I saw Wayne twice before I went away, but

everything was changed again between us. I was, on my side, no longer afraid or uneasy when I was with him and now, indeed, he appeared to avoid my company, taking obvious care not to be left alone with me. I do not know whether my grandfather spoke to him concerning me but I cannot believe that so sudden a change could have come about otherwise. Also, I did not know then that Red, with his knowledge of the stables and the Circuit and of everything sensual, had in the midst of the turmoil suspected that it was I and not Vinnie who had been concerned in the "accident" and had hinted at that to my grandfather. I did not know that, despite his apparent friendship and kinship with Wayne, he had always had a contempt for him, a contempt born of his own violent, direct nature for a sensualist more complex, more complicated and more perverse than himself. Looking back I am certain now that Red's one real love in life was horses and racing and that when he became restless and filled with desire he simply appeased the desire by any means at hand to end the torment and leave him free and undistracted in the pursuit of his real passion. He was a sturdy, healthy man and his torments were not feeble ones. His only real purpose was to clear them out of the way. That was really all women meant to him. There are many men like him who in their hearts regard all love with contempt and even hatred.

I did not know that Red had said to my grandfather in the heat of the first excitement on the afternoon of the "accident," "If you'll pardon my being frank, Judge, Wayne is a circular sonofabitch. He's a sonofabitch from every angle."

In any case I knew that I was no longer uneasy with Wayne and that from now on he could never touch me in any way and that very likely I would never see him again.

The afternoon of the day before I left to go back to school, the sheriff arrived suddenly at Clarendon. He went with my grandfather into his library and they remained there talking for a long time. The news of the arrival spread quickly and at the stables the colored folk got together in little groups gossiping and speculating. A little later Henry drove up, for the news which brought the sheriff had spread already through Masonville, and Henry on his way home from town had stopped to tell us.

It was that Emma Kleinfelter had confessed. It was she who had poisoned Old Virgil and Mattie.

The story was sordid enough. It came out in detail the next day when a hearing was held.

It seemed that they had tricked her into a confession by using another country girl as an *agent provocateur* when every other attempt to break down her defenses had failed, for Emma, like many dim-witted people, was extremely shrewd when it came to denying or hiding guilt. They had induced a girl called Verna Stebbins, the daughter of a neighboring farmer, to invite Emma over to spend the day, and during the hot afternoon the girls had gone to the haymow to lie in the hay and gossip and the girl had told Emma the fictitious story of a baffled love affair concocted between her and the sheriff and the prosecuting attorney. She told poor Emma that she was in love with a young neighbor and that her parents had forbidden her to marry him and that she had about decided to poison her parents so she could marry her lover. What, she asked Emma, did she think of the idea?

It was then that Emma's poor pride betrayed her. She boasted that that was exactly what she had already done. She had wanted to leave Old Virgil and Mattie to marry Red McGovern but Virgil wouldn't let her so she poisoned both of them. The sheriff's men, hiding in the mow, heard her tell all the story.

At the hearing the dim-witted girl betrayed a satisfaction in all the attention she received. Once she began telling her story there was no stopping her. She had, she said, obtained the arsenic by soaking it out of fly-paper (the old-fashioned sort that housewives put in a saucer of sweetened water) and then poured it into the *Schmierkäse*. She had soaked the arsenic out of a dozen packages of the stuff and then boiled it down. When, after breakfast on the fatal morning, Old Virgil and Mattie became violently ill, she did not go for the doctor at once but pretended to help them by giving them both warm water in which she put more arsenic. She was, she said, afraid that if she fetched the doctor they might recover. She only ran out and hailed my grandfather when she was sure that Mattie was dead and that Old Virgil was dying.

But that wasn't all she revealed. She told things at which my grandfather had guessed, the things that might have sent Old Virgil to jail and which my grandfather had intended to use in order to stop him spreading the story about Vinnie. She told of her seduction by the old man and of the beatings he had given her whenever he thought she had gone out to meet Red. The half-ruined, dirty old house had been an evil place indeed in which the concentrated hatred that dwelt there had exploded at last in poisoning and death.

The sheriff had come to see my grandfather as the best legal mind in the county about the legality of the way they had obtained the confession from the girl. Of course in the end the legality was not of much importance for it was clear that the girl was not responsible and that they could not send her to the penitentiary. They could only put her away in the asylum for the criminal insane.

In the excitement over the new sensation, the Valley forgot whatever gossip Old Virgil had been able to spread. And Wayne's "accident" was quickly forgotten. Aunt Susan had said that the stars seemed to have conspired together to bring disaster and tragedy to the Valley that summer, but really Aunt Susan was looking for an excuse to explain away the explosive events which seemed to have come all at once. The truth was that nothing of what happened had been an accident because the seeds of drama and tragedy had been there all the time and the pattern was little different from other patterns of drama and tragedy everywhere, a pattern in which love and avarice and lust and greed and poverty all played their roles. In a way the tragedy of Old Virgil and Mattie and the Kleinfelter girl had been in the making since the day Virgil was born and certainly from the day he married Mattie. Given that pattern, with the bandy-legged, lustful Red McGovern on a neighboring farm, disaster of some kind was the inevitable end to the story. The triangle of Henry, Vinnie and Wayne was as old as time itself.

Wayne left the day before I went away to school, and I think my grandfather was pleased to see him go and to know that he would not come back again into the Valley. My grandfather, I knew, would see him again and help him for he was not the sort to turn his back completely on someone who had once been his friend. I know that the relationship between them remained to the end a difficult and complex and complicated one, for while my grandfather could never wholly forgive him his behavior, he recognized too the fact that, although Wayne himself might never know or recognize or even be distressed by it, he was a lost and driven soul.

Wayne and I bade each other good-bye in a civilized and formal fashion, but I knew that although he no longer had any power to corrupt me or even to fill me with uneasiness, he was gone out of my life forever. And I knew that he had no longer any interest in me.

On Friday night I left and was at school on Monday morning but it was not the same school I had left in June of the same year. The buildings were the same and the headmaster and most of the teachers, and the routine was unchanged. It was different because I myself had changed, because out of the violence of the drama in which I found myself involved, I had grown up suddenly. The boys, even in the forms above me, seemed young and in some way incomplete as companions and their stories and talk of sex seemed puerile. I could not look at the teachers or even the head-master himself without wondering what their lives had been, or at least those parts of their lives which they chose to keep hidden away but which had so much to do with all the rest of existence.

Between the Grand Tour and meeting my grandmother and all that had happened in the Valley I had grown from a child to a man and so had crossed into the "wild country" that can be filled with the passion and torment, the confusion and distress which no child can ever know, or understand.

I saw Vinnie three weeks ago in the state capital where she had gone to be present at the inauguration of her son and my godson, Ronnie, as the newly elected governor of the state.

Much had happened in the years between. I myself was on the far borders of middle-age with children and grandchildren of my own. And Henry was dead of pneumonia at the age of sixty-eight. My grandfather and Aunt Susan were long in their graves in the family burial ground at Clarendon where they had lived out happily the last years of their lives; for after the death of Chastel a year from the time I had seen him in Salzburg, my grandmother came back to my grandfather, quietly and simply, as if nothing had happened.

I was at Clarendon when she returned. My grandfather went all the way to New York to meet her, returning with her on the train so that by the time they had reached Masonville the first inevitable strangeness had been worn away. Aunt Susan and I drove into Masonville in the surrey to meet them and when the train arrived my grandfather stepped out first and with great courtliness helped his wife down the high steps. On seeing us she came forward quickly, smiling, and bending down kissed Aunt Susan lightly on the cheek. It was an ordeal for Aunt Susan but she carried it off bravely, even gallantly, for she could never have approved of what had happened so long ago.

Then she turned quickly and kissed me in turn, saying, "My goodness, Ronnie. What a big fellow you are! You look just like your grandfather at your age!" And turning to my grandfather she said, "Can you remember back that far?"

He had been standing quietly by, smiling, and now he laughed. My grandfather smiled a great deal but one rarely heard him laugh. He was almost like a young man. As we moved across the platform to the surrey, my grandmother kept chattering, rather like one of Aunt Susan's gayer birds. There were no silences and no awkwardness. It was as if she and my grandfather had been away on a long journey and were delighted to be home again. The long ride back to Clarendon was like that all the way. Even Aunt Susan was forced to laugh aloud two or three times at the description of the voyage from Europe and the funny people on the boat.

It was my grandmother who carried off everything, and the remarkable thing was that she seemed as *right* here in the Valley as she had seemed in the Mirabelgarten in Salzburg with her blind, dying lover at her side. This, I think, was one of her great qualities—that she *belonged* wherever she found herself.

That night we had champagne for dinner and afterward she and my grandfather went out to the stables and paddocks to see the mares and the new foals. And afterward they visited the cabins and talked with the two or three old Negro stablemen whom she had known long ago as a bride and to all the new ones who had been born and grown up since she had last seen Clarendon. They, too, fell in love with her.

It was long after dark when the two of them finally returned to the house.

I think he knew all along that she would return to him although he waited for thirty years. He died first and after his death the two women went on spending their summers at Clarendon. With my wife and growing family, I returned there every year to spend a part of the summer with them. They sold off the horses, and Henry and Vinnie ran the farm for them. My older boys were about the same age as the younger boys of Henry and Vinnie and together with them Henry and I renewed our earlier expeditions through the swamps and into the Wild Country. When Aunt Susan died my grandmother went to live in Washington for good and died there at eighty-seven. To the end she remained a woman who was never lonely, for the Washington house was always filled with people all younger than herself who came to find what I had found that sunny day in the Mirabel restaurant in Salzburg a generation earlier. Whatever her sins, she remained to the end a pleasing woman who gave to the world much more than she demanded from it.

Wayne finally married the very nurse who had complained to my grandfather of his amorous attentions, but the marriage did not last for long. There was, I believe, some sort of scandal in Washington where with detectives she broke into a hotel room and found him with her best friend. At any rate the story came back to his home state and was true enough to ruin his political career and force him into the insurance business. I saw him once in Miami Beach as a man of fifty-five. The big, good looks had coarsened; he was heavy and gross in appearance and a little drunk. It was hard to believe that all the good looks, the fair skin, the great health and vitality had changed so greatly. With him was a woman of thirty or thirty-five, quite obviously a five-dollar chippy.

He was buying now what once he had used his good looks and charm unscrupulously to obtain. Perhaps this was the retribution my grandfather had in mind. He had lived by the flesh without other resources and now the flesh was failing him there was nowhere to turn. Fortunately he did not see me.

In the governor's suite at the hotel in the state capital, Vinnie and I had outstayed all the others who had come to the reception, even the greedy, little politicians who swarmed about seeking jobs for themselves and their friends and relations. It was nearly four in the morning when the Governor—"her" Ronnie—and Vinnie and I found ourselves alone in a room filled with smoke, cigarette butts and empty glasses and bottles.

She always referred to her eldest son as "my" Ronnie to distinguish him from me. He was a good-looking fellow who resembled Henry more than herself with much of the physical radiance which Henry himself had possessed as a young man. But he looked tired now and Vinnie said, "Go on to bed, son. Ronnie and I want to talk. You've had a hard day."

He bade us good night and as he left the room there returned to me the fleeting impression I had had long ago as a boy at school when I received the news of his birth that somehow I had had something to do with his existence.

When the door closed, I looked at Vinnie and asked, "Proud of him?" And she smiled and said, with the faint accent she had never wholly lost, "Sure I am. What you think?" And between us there passed a quick flash of understanding which seemed to encompass all the years of our association since the day when I had heard Old Virgil say, "Henry's brung himself home a chippy."

The sense of strain and guilt which we once shared had long since vanished and we had reached that stage in life where we could, as my grandfather had done in his day, see life in the whole through a long perspective in which we judge people and their actions not by any rigid and arbitrary code but in terms of humanity and in some degree of pity and humor and tolerance, seeing that perhaps even the evil ones could not have done much to save themselves since the pattern of their existence is often enough determined by forces which no man can properly control.

Vinnie had fought for integrity and security with her quiet love and respect for Henry's goodness, against forces which I had learned to understand and fear even as a boy. And she had won her battle, preserving his farm and his existence and his love for her. She had borne and raised for him four sons and two daughters and helped him to become one of the richest farmers in the state. She had made herself one of the most respected women in the Valley, even in the state. I doubt that anyone remained alive who remembered anything of Old Virgil's malice and gossip.

I do not know whether Henry ever found out about what had happened on the grassy ledge of the Wild Country or whether he ever really knew anything of her sordid, tragic life in St. Louis before he married her. There was never any sign of his knowing but as my grandfather had said, he would have been the last to hear. But one could never tell with a man like Henry, not because he was complex and subtle, but because he had always been so simple that he may have known much more than either of us suspected. He may have judged for himself and decided that what Vinnie had outweighed many times the mistakes she may have made; and being a simple man he may have understood instinctively and more clearly than any of us the devastating form of the passion for Wayne of that other Vinnie whom he himself never knew. In any case he had had no reason to complain. He had been happy and he worshipped her to the end of his life and together with her he had built up perhaps the best of all lives close to the earth with good and healthy children and happiness in his land and his animals and pride in his wife and in what they had built together out of their own spirits with their own hands.

And now Vinnie sat there, her once-dyed and brassy hair now grey, with a strong, solid body which had thickened a little with the bearing of many children. Her face had not changed much because of the beautiful bone structure that was a heritage of her Polish blood. In some ways she had grown more beautiful as she had grown older, perhaps because as fear left her and the security she had hungered for became a reality, there was no longer any fear to darken her spirit and dampen the humor which increased with age. The only lines in her otherwise smooth face were those which came from much smiling and laughing.

I remembered the night before I left for school when she had come up to my room with the cookies and the milk and I know now, as indeed I had known long ago, that she was aware of what she was doing, perhaps instinctively, perhaps with design; she had come up the stairs of the old house to help a lonely and confused boy to find his way into manhood. In a way it seemed to me that she knew everything and had always known everything even long ago when she had fought, terrified, to preserve what she knew was good and, more than that, was solid and enduring.

Now that we were alone we found we had very little to talk about. What we had not thrashed out long ago was beyond talk and I knew that in any case we understood those things and had no need for talking of them. She put down her glass of Bourbon on the arm of her chair and a twinkle came into her clear, grey-blue eyes.

"I wish I had my accordion here," she said, "I would sink you some sad sonks!"

Set in Intertype Garamond
Format by A. W. Rushmore
Manufactured by The Haddon Craftsmen
Published by HARPER & BROTHERS, *New York*